OPPOSING
VIEWPOINTS®
SERIES

Genetically Modified Foods and the Global Food Supply

Other Books of Related Interest

Opposing Viewpoints Series

Corporate Farming
Global Sustainability
Pesticides and GMOs
The Politics of Water Scarcity

At Issue Series

Environmental Racism and Classism
Foodborne Outbreaks
Food Security
The Role of Science in Public Policy

Current Controversies Series

Agriculture
Environmental Catastrophe
Genetic Engineering
The Industrial Food Complex

> "Congress shall make no law … abridging the freedom of speech, or of the press."

First Amendment to the US Constitution

The basic foundation of our democracy is the First Amendment guarantee of freedom of expression. The Opposing Viewpoints series is dedicated to the concept of this basic freedom and the idea that it is more important to practice it than to enshrine it.

**OPPOSING
VIEWPOINTS®
SERIES**

Genetically Modified Foods and the Global Food Supply

Avery Elizabeth Hurt, Book Editor

GREENHAVEN
PUBLISHING

Published in 2022 by Greenhaven Publishing, LLC
353 3rd Avenue, Suite 255, New York, NY 10010

Cover image: LEDOMSTOCK/Shutterstock.com

Library of Congress Cataloging-in-Publication Data

Names: Hurt, Avery Elizabeth, editor.
Title: Genetically modified foods and the global food supply / Avery
 Elizabeth Hurt.
Description: New York : Greenhaven Publishing, 2022. | Series: Opposing
 viewpoints | Includes bibliographical references and index. | Audience: Grades 9–12.
Identifiers: LCCN 2020001668 | ISBN 9781534506879 (library binding) | ISBN
 9781534506862 (paperback)
Subjects: LCSH: Genetically modified foods—Juvenile literature. |
 Genetically modified foods—Environmental aspects—Juvenile literature.
 | Genetically modified foods—Economic aspects—Juvenile literature. |
 Genetically modified foods—Health aspects—Juvenile literature. | Food
 supply—Environmental aspects—Juvenile literature. | Food
 supply—Economic aspects—Juvenile literature.
Classification: LCC TP248.65.F66 G4579 2022 | DDC 664—dc23
LC record available at https://lccn.loc.gov/2020001668

Manufactured in the United States of America

Website: http://greenhavenpublishing.com

Contents

The Importance of Opposing Viewpoints   **11**

Introduction   **14**

Chapter 1: Are Genetically Modified Foods Safe to Eat?

Chapter Preface   **18**

1. Genetically Modified Foods Need Better Regulation   **19**
   Dana Perls

2. GMOs Can Provide Benefits for Developing Nations   **25**
   Ramez Naam

3. We Need to Err on the Side of Caution   **33**
   Melis Ann

4. GMO Products May Cause Cancer   **40**
   Jeffrey Smith

5. We Need a Better Approach to Regulating Genetically Modified Crops   **45**
   Matin Qaim

6. Commercially Available GMOs Are Safe to Eat   **51**
   Editors of Best Food Facts

Periodical and Internet Sources Bibliography   **57**

Chapter 2: Do Genetically Modified Crops Pose a Danger to the Environment?

Chapter Preface   **60**

1. A Genetically Modified Crop Is Loose and Evolving   **61**
   David Biello

2. GMOs Are Better for the Environment Than You Probably Think   **65**
   Marco Giovannetti

3. GMOs Pose Several Serious Environmental Concerns   **70**
   Shirley Martin-Abel

4. Regenerative Agriculture Can Undo the Harms of   75
    Traditional Agriculture
    Kate Spring
5. GMO Technology Should Be Transferred to the   80
    Developing World
    Luis R. Herrera-Estrella
Periodical and Internet Sources Bibliography   88

Chapter 3: Are Genetically Modified Foods Necessary to Feed the World's Growing Population?

Chapter Preface   90
1. Genetically Engineered Foods Can Save Lives   91
    Daniel Norero
2. GMOs Are Not Necessary to Feed the World   96
    Green America
3. GMO Crops May Help Solve Problems Created by   101
    Climate Change
    Stuart Thompson
4. GM Crops Won't Help African Farmers   106
    Million Belay
5. The Complex Problem of Food Scarcity Will Need   110
    an Equally Complex Solution
    Genetic Literacy Project
6. GMOs Can Feed the World, but We Need to   117
    Develop the Right Crops
    Paul Diehl
Periodical and Internet Sources Bibliography   121

Chapter 4: Is Increased Corporate Control of the Food System a Dangerous Idea?

Chapter Preface   **123**

1. Corporate Control of Farming Is the Real Point of   **124**
   GM Food
   Colin Tudge

2. Real People, Not Faceless Multinationals, Should   **135**
   Feed the World
   John Vidal

3. Transparency in Labeling Laws Can Help Create   **140**
   Acceptance of GM Foods
   Katherine McComas, Graham Dixon, and John C. Besley

4. Even If GMOs Are Safe, Mandatory Labeling Is a   **145**
   Good Idea
   Mahni Ghorashi

5. GM Foods Serve Corporate Greed, Not Human Need   **152**
   Ghiselle Karim

6. GM Crops Are a Valuable Tool in Addressing Global   **158**
   Poverty
   Mark Tester

Periodical and Internet Sources Bibliography   **162**

For Further Discussion   **164**

Organizations to Contact   **166**

Bibliography of Books   **171**

Index   **173**

The Importance of Opposing Viewpoints

Perhaps every generation experiences a period in time in which the populace seems especially polarized, starkly divided on the important issues of the day and gravitating toward the far ends of the political spectrum and away from a consensus-facilitating middle ground. The world that today's students are growing up in and that they will soon enter into as active and engaged citizens is deeply fragmented in just this way. Issues relating to terrorism, immigration, women's rights, minority rights, race relations, health care, taxation, wealth and poverty, the environment, policing, military intervention, the proper role of government—in some ways, perennial issues that are freshly and uniquely urgent and vital with each new generation—are currently roiling the world.

If we are to foster a knowledgeable, responsible, active, and engaged citizenry among today's youth, we must provide them with the intellectual, interpretive, and critical-thinking tools and experience necessary to make sense of the world around them and of the all-important debates and arguments that inform it. After all, the outcome of these debates will in large measure determine the future course, prospects, and outcomes of the world and its peoples, particularly its youth. If they are to become successful members of society and productive and informed citizens, students need to learn how to evaluate the strengths and weaknesses of someone else's arguments, how to sift fact from opinion and fallacy, and how to test the relative merits and validity of their own opinions against the known facts and the best possible available information. The landmark series Opposing Viewpoints has been providing students with just such critical-thinking skills and exposure to the debates surrounding society's most urgent contemporary issues for many years, and it continues to serve this essential role with undiminished commitment, care, and rigor.

The key to the series's success in achieving its goal of sharpening students' critical-thinking and analytic skills resides in its title—

Opposing Viewpoints. In every intriguing, compelling, and engaging volume of this series, readers are presented with the widest possible spectrum of distinct viewpoints, expert opinions, and informed argumentation and commentary, supplied by some of today's leading academics, thinkers, analysts, politicians, policy makers, economists, activists, change agents, and advocates. Every opinion and argument anthologized here is presented objectively and accorded respect. There is no editorializing in any introductory text or in the arrangement and order of the pieces. No piece is included as a "straw man," an easy ideological target for cheap point-scoring. As wide and inclusive a range of viewpoints as possible is offered, with no privileging of one particular political ideology or cultural perspective over another. It is left to each individual reader to evaluate the relative merits of each argument— as he or she sees it, and with the use of ever-growing critical-thinking skills—and grapple with his or her own assumptions, beliefs, and perspectives to determine how convincing or successful any given argument is and how the reader's own stance on the issue may be modified or altered in response to it.

This process is facilitated and supported by volume, chapter, and selection introductions that provide readers with the essential context they need to begin engaging with the spotlighted issues, with the debates surrounding them, and with their own perhaps shifting or nascent opinions on them. In addition, guided reading and discussion questions encourage readers to determine the authors' point of view and purpose, interrogate and analyze the various arguments and their rhetoric and structure, evaluate the arguments' strengths and weaknesses, test their claims against available facts and evidence, judge the validity of the reasoning, and bring into clearer, sharper focus the reader's own beliefs and conclusions and how they may differ from or align with those in the collection or those of their classmates.

Research has shown that reading comprehension skills improve dramatically when students are provided with compelling, intriguing, and relevant "discussable" texts. The subject matter of these collections could not be more compelling, intriguing, or urgently relevant to today's students and the world they are poised to inherit. The anthologized articles and the reading and discussion questions that are included with them also provide the basis for stimulating, lively, and passionate classroom debates. Students who are compelled to anticipate objections to their own argument and identify the flaws in those of an opponent read more carefully, think more critically, and steep themselves in relevant context, facts, and information more thoroughly. In short, using discussable text of the kind provided by every single volume in the Opposing Viewpoints series encourages close reading, facilitates reading comprehension, fosters research, strengthens critical thinking, and greatly enlivens and energizes classroom discussion and participation. The entire learning process is deepened, extended, and strengthened.

For all of these reasons, Opposing Viewpoints continues to be exactly the right resource at exactly the right time—when we most need to provide readers with the critical-thinking tools and skills that will not only serve them well in school but also in their careers and their daily lives as decision-making family members, community members, and citizens. This series encourages respectful engagement with and analysis of opposing viewpoints and fosters a resulting increase in the strength and rigor of one's own opinions and stances. As such, it helps make readers "future ready," and that readiness will pay rich dividends for the readers themselves, for the citizenry, for our society, and for the world at large.

Introduction

*"It's often alleged that GM is not
natural. Well, orthodox agriculture is
not natural, it's extremely damaging
to the environment and if GM crops
can be produced that require less
herbicide, or pesticide, or water,
then I think we as a society have
to understand that there are some
benefits involved."*

—*Richard Deverell,
director of Britain's Royal
Botanic Gardens at Kew*

Almost every bite of food you eat has been genetically modified by humans. Humans have been tinkering with the genetics of organisms for at least thirty thousand years, breeding plants and animals to get the traits they wanted. It's how humans turned wolves into poodles and a wild grass with a few small seeds into a fat ear of corn studded with golden kernels. Farmers select plants and animals with useful characteristics (a tomato that can hold up to excessive heat, a cow that gives plenty of milk) and then breed them. In the next generation, they pick out the plants or animals that have inherited these preferred traits and breed them. After years of this selective breeding, hardy tomatoes and productive cows become the norm. Most of the foods we eat today bear little resemblance to their natural ancestors. They've been much changed and improved to suit human need and desires.

No one finds this alarming. However, something changed in the late twentieth century. Humans discovered a totally new—and much faster—way to tinker with their food. In 1954, James Watson and Francis Crick, with the help of scientists Rosalind Franklin and Maurice Williams and Linus Pauling, not to mention earlier scientists whose work the duo built upon, figured out the structure of DNA, the carrier of genetic material. It didn't take long for other scientists to learn how to alter it. By 1972, scientists had figured out how to snip genes out of the DNA of one organism and insert them into the DNA of another organism. This was genetic tinkering on a whole new level. The technique was soon used to alter foods, create medicines, and even alter the DNA of animals.

One of the most common uses for this new biotechnology is to insert into soybeans a gene that makes it resistant to glyphosate, an herbicide made by a chemical company called Monsanto. (Monsanto has since been purchased by Bayer, a German pharmaceutical company.) This makes it possible for farmers to treat a field for weeds using glyphosate knowing that the herbicide will kill weeds, but not kill their soybean crop. This made it easier and cheaper for farmers to control weeds and grow high-yielding crops. It also made it possible, thanks to the US Supreme Court, for Monsanto to patent these resistant seeds. Before long, other crops were genetically modified to make them more productive, disease resistant, or in some cases more nutritious. In one famous case, an apple has been altered simply to keep it from turning brown after it is cut.

The public responded to the genetic modification of their food supply with more than a little suspicion. After at least thirty years of research on these foods, there are still questions about their safety. Many scientists claim that genetically modified (GM) foods are perfectly safe to eat. Others aren't so sure. The public has a difficult time getting answers they can trust. Many of the studies showing genetically modified organisms (GMOs) are safe have been funded by companies or conducted by researchers who stand to gain from the adoption of these crops. On the other hand, some of the loudest critics of the technology seem to some a bit too passionate about the issue to be completely trustworthy. The arguments on both sides can sometimes seem driven more by a baked-in opinion about the technology than to a careful analysis of the evidence. It would seem to be a reasonable compromise to simply require food companies to clearly label any foods that contain GMOs. However, it turns out that if these foods are labeled, the public is less likely to buy them. Even if they don't know exactly why, many people would just prefer to err on the side of caution and not eat GMOs.

Food safety is only one of the problems, however. Growing GM crops potentially poses risks to the environment. Or, depending on who you ask, these crops could potentially help save the environment from the effects of climate change. Crops that can thrive under drought conditions, for example, might save millions from starvation in the coming years. The risks and benefits are still a matter of debate. A great deal is at stake.

There are also social and economic aspects to the argument. Is it really a good idea to let huge agricultural companies own the patents to seeds, to give them virtual control of the planet's food supply? How do small farmers survive in a world where agriculture is controlled by multinational corporations? Some say the problem is overblown; others are deeply concerned.

Opposing Viewpoints: Genetically Modified Foods and the Global Food Supply offers many different takes on these and other issues surrounding this new development of a very old practice. In chapters titled "Are Genetically Modified Foods Safe to Eat?" "Do Genetically Modified Crops Pose a Danger to the Environment?" "Are Genetically Modified Foods Necessary to Feed the World's Growing Population?" and "Is Increased Corporate Control of the Food System a Dangerous Idea?" you will read perspectives of scientists, policy makers, and concerned citizens, among others. Some believe GM foods are dangerous, while others think they are the only hope for feeding a rapidly growing world. All of them, in one way or another, are seeking the best way to feed the people of the world while keeping humans and the environment healthy.

OPPOSING
VIEWPOINTS®
SERIES

CHAPTER 1

Are Genetically Modified Foods Safe to Eat?

Chapter Preface

There are many questions about the effects of genetically modified organisms, but for most people, the primary concern is health. Are these new foods safe to eat? For many, the idea of people with test tubes and centrifuges tinkering with something as basic as the food we put in our mouths sounds like something out of science fiction. In fact, detractors of GM foods often call them Frankenfoods, a reference to the novel *Frankenstein* by Mary Shelley. When the book's Dr. Frankenstein tried to tinker with natural life, he created a monster. Are we now finding monsters on our plates?

Though the idea of genetically modified food can be creepy, there has been little evidence that it is dangerous. However, cautious types point out that absence of evidence is not evidence of absence. It could be that the harms have not yet shown themselves. Also, there is the fact that the harms may not be what health inspectors are looking for. For example, the herbicide glyphosate (one common trade name is Roundup) is not a food, but it is a part of the genetic manipulation of agriculture and often shows up even in foods that are not genetically modified. The debate about the safety of glyphosate is still raging, even among those who admit that most genetically modified foods pose little harm in and of themselves.

The viewpoints in this chapter attempt to address some of the nuances of these arguments. Some authors seem completely convinced that there is no reason to worry about GM foods; others sound the alarm with vigor. Some cite scientific research; others rely mostly on hearsay or assumptions. And no one side of the issue has a monopoly on sloppy reasoning or unfounded claims. If you read the following viewpoints with care and attention, you may not find yourself coming to a firm conclusion on the issue of genetically modified foods. But you likely will learn a lot about the issues involved and how the public debate is unfolding.

> *"Researchers are tinkering with nature's DNA in new and potentially problematic ways and without clear regulatory guidance."*

Genetically Modified Foods Need Better Regulation

Dana Perls

In the following viewpoint, Dana Perls explains what she calls the next generation of genetically modified organisms—foods that are beginning to appear in supermarkets and restaurants. Because of potential risks and consumer concerns, she calls for better regulation and labelling of these foods. Dana Perls is the senior food and agriculture campaigner with Friends of the Earth and leads the Food and Agriculture team's international and national regulatory and market campaigns on biotechnology and genetic engineering.

As you read, consider the following questions:

1. How are researchers able to alter a species, according to this viewpoint?
2. How are companies able to call these altered species "natural," according to Perl?
3. What criticisms does the author have of the "apple that never browns"?

"Next-Generation Genetically Modified Foods Need Better Regulation," by Dana Perls, STAT, February 2, 2017. Reprinted by permission.

The apple that never browns wants to change your mind about genetically modified foods."

That headline in the *Washington Post* is just one of many shining the spotlight on the next generation of genetically modified organisms (what many are calling GMO 2.0) heading to our supermarkets and restaurants.

Gene-silenced Arctic apples that do not turn brown when exposed to air, even when rotten, will be sold in stores in the Midwest this week. Other products on the way include canola oil extracted from rapeseed that has been modified by gene editing to withstand more pesticides, but which is being marketed as a non-GMO food by its maker; salmon genetically engineered with eel genes to grow faster; and synthetic vanillin excreted from genetically modified yeast, yet marketed as "natural."

Researchers are tinkering with nature's DNA in new and potentially problematic ways and without clear regulatory guidance. They can alter a species by editing or deleting genes, turning genes on or off, or even creating completely new DNA sequences on a computer. Some of these new foods will be marketed as "non-GMO" or "natural" because the definition of GMO has not yet caught up with the pace of new biotechnology developments.

Existing definitions focus on *transgenic* technologies that take genes from one species and put them into another. But many companies are modifying organisms' genomes without adding another organisms's genes using gene-silencing techniques such as RNA interference and gene-editing techniques such as CRISPR.

New GMO foods are being released with little understanding of their potential health and environmental consequences. So far, no safety assessments specific to these new techniques are required, and no regulatory oversight is in place for this swiftly moving set of new technologies.

To address that gap in regulations, the Department of Agriculture recently announced a proposal for updating its biotechnology regulations. While it is good that the USDA is considering regulating gene-edited foods, the proposal is riddled with loopholes that could exclude many new GMO foods. I believe that all genetically engineered crops, including ones made with gene-editing tools like CRISPR, should be regulated and assessed for health and environmental impacts.

Biotech companies in this emerging market hope consumers are attracted to new GMO products. Intrexon, the company that makes the non-browning GMO Arctic apple, believes that this product may lead to less food waste. Yet there's a reason an apple turns brown—it's a signal it has been cut or bruised. If a little oxidizing is worrisome, we can use lemon juice, a proven, natural method to prevent it. Some scientists believe apples' natural browning enzyme may help fight diseases and pests, meaning that farmers may have to increase their pesticide use to grow non-browning apples.

Research also suggests that newer technologies such as gene silencing may pose health risks, and some of the genetic material used, such as double-stranded RNA, could affect gene expression in human cells in ways that have not yet been investigated.

The first generation of GMOs was promoted to reduce pesticide use in agriculture. Yet data show that the widespread use of GMO crops has actually *increased* the use of glyphosate-based Roundup herbicide. Not only are there serious environmental consequences associated with such an increase, but the International Agency for Research on Cancer recently declared that glyphosate is a probable human carcinogen, and a recent long-term study linked low doses of Roundup to serious liver damage.

We understand even less about the potential unintended impacts of GMO 2.0 foods. It is unclear how these new technologies might evolve once released into the environment; how they might interact with their ecosystems; and whether they might result in permanent changes to other organisms or ecosystems.

Although some experts suggest that gene-editing techniques like CRISPR are more precise than the first-generation genetic engineering technologies, there are still documented off-target effects, meaning they will likely have unintended consequences. CRISPR will probably be used to produce more herbicide-tolerant

Genetically Engineered Foods Must Be Clearly Labeled

The genetic engineering of plants and animals is looming as one of the greatest and most intractable environmental challenges of the 21st Century.

Currently, up to 92% of US corn is genetically engineered (GE), as are 94% of soybeans and 94% of cotton (cottonseed oil is often used in food products). It has been estimated that upwards of 75% of processed foods on supermarket shelves—from soda to soup, crackers to condiments—contain genetically engineered ingredients.

By removing the genetic material from one organism and inserting it into the permanent genetic code of another, the biotech industry has created an astounding number of organisms that are not produced by nature and have never been seen on the plate. These include potatoes with bacteria genes, "super" pigs with human growth genes, fish with cattle growth genes, tomatoes with flounder genes, corn with bacteria genes, and thousands of other altered and engineered plants, animals and insects. At an alarming rate, these creations are now being patented and released into our environment and our food supply.

A number of studies over the past decade have revealed that genetically engineered foods can pose serious risks to farmers, human health, domesticated animals, wildlife and the environment. Despite these long-term and wide-ranging risks, Congress has yet to pass a single law intended to manage them responsibly. The haphazard and negligent agency regulation of biotechnology has been a disaster for consumers and the environment. Unsuspecting consumers by the tens of millions are purchasing and consuming unlabeled GE foods, despite a finding by US Food & Drug Administration scientists that these foods could pose serious risks.

Center for Food Safety seeks to halt the approval, commercialization and/or release of any new genetically engineered crops until they have been thoroughly tested and found safe for human health and the environment. CFS maintains that any foods that already contain GE ingredients must be clearly labeled, and advocates for the containment and reduction of existing genetically engineered crops.

"About Genetically Engineered Foods," The Center for Food Safety.

GMOs, which will perpetuate the toxic treadmill of increased chemical dependency in agriculture, taking us further away from healthy food systems.

There are also serious sustainability concerns with GMO 2.0 foods. For example, using genetically modified yeast to make vanillin requires vast amounts of feedstock—the sugary broth used to grow yeast. Common feedstocks, usually from corn or sugar cane, are typically produced in chemical-intensive industrial agricultural systems.

GMO 2.0 foods could also affect millions of small sustainable farmers around the world whose livelihoods depend on growing the valuable natural crops that will be replaced. Many synthetic biology products are intended to replace plant-based commodities typically grown in developing countries, such as vanilla, saffron, cacao, coconut, shea butter, stevia, and others. This raises serious questions about who will benefit from the production of these new technologies and who will bear the costs. A holistic analysis of sustainability—which hasn't yet been done—would likely point to the many environmental and social shortcomings of this next generation of biotechnologies.

Fortunately, food companies and retailers are listening to consumer demand. Fast food companies like McDonald's and Wendy's have said they will not carry the GMO apple. More than 60 major grocery stores, including Walmart, Costco, Albertsons, and others, have committed not to carry the GMO salmon.

The Non-GMO Project and the National Organic Standards Board have made it clear that GMO 2.0 technologies like gene silencing and CRISPR are, indeed, genetic engineering techniques that must not be used in the production and manufacture of any product carrying the Non-GMO Verified or USDA Organic labels. Now it's time for the US government to add its voice to the issue. We need more science, assessment, answers, and regulations before we can decide whether these new biotech products should be in our stores—and on our plates. Instead, we are being kept in the dark, with no clue about what foods contain these unlabeled ingredients.

There is widespread consumer concern about GMOs and genetically modified foods. Friends of the Earth is working with various allies to educate the public about the next generation of GMOs. Instead of being swayed by Intrexon's narrative of the value of non-browning GMO Arctic apples, we want food that is truly natural, sustainable, organic, and healthy.

> *"GMOs are neither poison nor panacea. What they are is a toolkit, a varied one, with real benefits to the environment and millions of people today."*

GMOs Can Provide Benefits for Developing Nations

Ramez Naam

In the previous viewpoint, the author was concerned about the potential risks of genetically modified foods sold in supermarkets in the developed world. In the following viewpoint, Ramez Naam explores the issue from a very different point of view. GMOs, the author argues, will not make a huge difference in the developed world, one way or the other, but they could be a game changer for countries struggling to feed their populations. Ramez Naam is an American technologist and author of The Infinite Resource: The Power of Ideas on a Finite Planet.

"Why GMOs Matter—Especially for the Developing World," by Ramez Naam, Grist Magazine, Inc., January 22, 2014. Reprinted by permission.

As you read, consider the following questions:

1. What are some of the advantages of GM crops mentioned here, and how might those, according to the author, outweigh the risks?
2. How does the author describe the effect of genetically modified crops in developing areas, such as India, the Philippines, and African nations?
3. How does the author counter the argument that GMOs are contributing to farmer suicides in India?

The folks at Grist have kindly allowed me to pen a guest post here with a few thoughts on Nathanael Johnson's excellent series on genetically modified foods and in particular his most recent piece on what he learned from 6 months investigating the GMO debate: that none of it really matters.

This most recent piece nails several key points that often go completely missed. When we get down to the specifics, we find that today's GMOs are neither planetary panacea nor unbridled poison. The passionate, emotion-filled debate is more about the lenses through which we see the world as it is about genetically modified foods themselves. The GMO debate is often an emphatic and barely-disguised metaphor for our larger debate about whether technology is destroying the world or saving it, whether we should try to control nature or live within it.

That's not to say the debate, when it touches on GMOs themselves, is balanced. The scientific consensus is that GMOs are as safe to eat as any other food, that they reduce soil-damaging tillage, reduce carbon emissions, reduce insecticide use, and reduce the use of the most toxic herbicides in favor of far milder ones. GMOs have limitations, and some of their benefits are threatened by the rise of pesticide resistance. Even so, on balance, GMOs are safe and produce real benefits. As I wrote at Discover Magazine last year, GMOs achieve many of the goals of organic agriculture.

(To balance that out, let me state that I also wrote there that GMO supporters should embrace sensible GMO labeling.)

But Johnson is also right that, in the US, the stakes are not at present world-changing. US farmers could likely get by without GMOs. We might see upticks in toxic pesticide use and river runoffs, in soil-harming tillage, and in carbon emissions, but none of those would prove catastrophic. There might be a very slight reduction in crop yield, but not by much, and not for long. The vast majority of us would never notice.

In that context, I agree that the current debate is more about abstractions, metaphors, and worldviews than it is about the realities on the ground.

Even so, I think there are two important reasons we should care about GMOs, and view them, certainly not as panaceas, but as imperfect but important tools that can improve the lives of millions of people right now and possibly have an impact on billions of lives and millions of square miles of nature in the decades to come.

Why We Should Care—The Long Term

The Food and Agriculture Organization of the UN estimates that we need to grow 70 percent more food by 2050. Either we do this on the same land we have today, or we chop down forest to create farms and pastures to meet that demand, something no one wants to do.

Jon Foley at the Institute on the Environment points out, quite rightly, that it's meat consumption, not population, that's driving global food demand. So we could, instead, reduce meat consumption. That's a noble goal. Unfortunately, meat consumption has roughly quadrupled in the last 50 years, primarily driven by increasing wealth in the developing world, with no sign of stopping. I welcome any practical plan to reduce meat consumption worldwide, but until then, we have to find a way to keep boosting food production.

Another way to feed the world is to close the "yield gap" between farms in the rich and poor worlds. Farmers in the US grow twice as much food per acre as the world overall, largely because they can afford farm equipment, fuel, fertilizer, and pesticides that many farmers in the developing world can't. Some of this gap, undoubtedly, will be closed as poverty drops around the world. But it's unrealistic to assume that all of it will.

What are we to do? On the horizon are some GMOs in development that could provide a dramatic boost here.

1. **Better photosynthesis. Corn and sugarcane grow** nearly twice as much food per acre as the crops humans eat most: rice and wheat. Why? Corn and sugarcane have a better way of doing photosynthesis—of turning light, plus water, plus CO2 into carbohydrates. This newer system is called C4 photosynthesis. Researchers around the world—funded by nonprofits like the Gates Foundation—are working on creating C4 Rice and C4 Wheat. Those crops could grow 50 percent more food per acre.

2. **Self-fertilizing crops.** Fertilizer boosts plant growth by adding nitrogen, and access to fertilizer is one reason rich nation farms grow so much more food per acre than their developing world counterparts. But fertilizer runoff is also responsible for the Gulf dead zone and similar zones around the world. Some crops, though, can fertilize themselves by pulling nitrogen from the air. Legumes, like soy, peas, and clover do this. Another nonprofit funded GMO research area is to transfer this ability to cereal crops, creating self-fertilizing wheat, corn, and rice. That would have two advantages: It would boost yields for poor farmers who can't afford additional fertilizer; and it would cut down on nitrogen runoff that creates these ocean dead zones.

These are just two projects among many, along with creating more drought-resistant crops, more salt-resistant crops, and crops that have higher levels of vitamins and minerals that people need.

Now, let me be very clear. Most of these are research projects. They're not in the here and now. They're not going to arrive this year, and probably not in the next 10 years. And we do continue to make great progress in improving crops through conventional breeding. But we're unlikely to ever get to, say, C4 rice or C4 wheat through conventional breeding.

The bigger point here isn't that we absolutely need GMOs to feed the future world. If we banned all future GMO development and planting, we'd most likely muddle through in some way. Humanity is good at innovating, particularly when our back is to the wall. But we'd be fighting this battle to keep increasing food output with one arm tied behind our back. We might make less progress in boosting yields, without GMOs, meaning food prices would be higher, hunger would be higher, or we'd have more pressure to chop down forests to grow food.

Or maybe we'd be just fine. But given the size of the challenge, and the absence of any credible evidence of harm from GMOs, robbing ourselves of this part of our toolkit strikes me as foolish.

Why We Should Care—The Here and Now

The future's easy to discount. So let's come back to the present, and in particular, the present reality for the 6 billion people who live outside of the rich world.

Until recently, the majority of the acres of GM farmland in the world have been in rich nations. Today, the US ranks first, followed by Brazil and Argentina (what we'd call middle income nations), and then Canada (another rich nation). That means that when we look at how GM crops perform, we tend to focus on how they do in countries where farmers have access to farm equipment, fertilizer, pesticides, irrigation, and so on. And in those countries we see a real but modest benefit.

In the developing world, it's markedly different.

India allows only one genetically modified crop: GM cotton with the Bt trait, which makes the cotton naturally resistant to insects and reduces the need to spray insecticides. In the US, there's a broad consensus that Bt corn has reduced insecticide spraying (which is good) but less evidence that it's increased how much food is actually produced per acre, at least to a significant degree. In India, where quite a large number of farmers can't readily afford pesticides, and where they lack farm equipment, meaning that pesticides must be applied by hand, the situation is dramatically different.

For the decade between 1991 and 2001, cotton yields in India were flat, at around 300 kilograms per hectare (a hectare is about 2.5 acres). In 2002, Bt cotton was introduced into the country. Farmers adopted it quickly, and yields of cotton soared by *two thirds* in just a few years to more than 500 kilograms per hectare.

Between 1975 and 2009, researchers found that Bt cotton produced 19 percent of India's yield growth, despite the fact that it was only on the market for 8 of those 24 years. The simpler view is that Bt cotton, in India, lifts yields by somewhere between 50 percent and 70 percent.

Why does this matter? There are 7 million cotton farmers in India. Several peer reviewed studies have found that, because Bt cotton increases the amount of crop they have to sell, it raises their farm profits by as much as 50 percent, helps lift them out of poverty and reduces their risk of falling into hunger. By reducing the amount of insecticide used (which, in India, is mostly sprayed by hand) Bt cotton has also massively reduced insecticide poisoning to farm workers there—to the tune of 2.4 million cases per year.

You may perhaps be wondering: Don't GMOs lead to more farmer suicides in India? And while farmer suicides in India are real, and each one is a tragedy, the link is false. Farmer suicides have been going on long before GMOs, and, if anything, the farmer suicide rate has slightly dropped since the introduction of GM seeds.

In China we've seen similar impacts of Bt cotton, with multiple studies showing that Bt cotton increased yields, boosted the incomes of 4 million smallholder farmers, and reduced pesticide poisoning among them.

All of this is to say that GM crops have more impact in poor countries than rich ones. Where other types of inputs, like fertilizers, farm equipment, and pesticides are harder to afford, GM crops have more to offer. That can help increase food, reduce pressure on deforestation, and lift farmers out of poverty.

But the world's poorest countries, and in particular India and the bulk of sub-Saharan Africa, don't allow any GM *food crops* to be grown. India came close to approval for a Bt eggplant (or Bt brinjal). Studies showed that it was safe, that it could cut pesticide use by half, and that it could nearly double yields by reducing losses to insects. But, while India's regulators approved the planting and sale, activists cried out, prompting the government to place an indefinite moratorium on it. Similar things have happened elsewhere. The same Bt eggplant was supported by regulators in the Philippines who looked at the data, but then blocked by the court on grounds that reflected not specific concerns, but general, metaphorical, and emotional arguments that Nathanael Johnson describes as dominating the debate.

That's a pity. Because if Bt food crops could produce similar size gains in the developing world, that would be a tremendous benefit. Insect losses are a tremendously larger challenge in India and Africa than in the US. Boosting the amount of food that a farm produces by half or more means less hunger, more income for farmers (still the majority of the population in the world's poorest countries), and more ability of people to pull themselves out of poverty.

The same arguments that kept Bt eggplant out of the Philippines have also been used, often by western groups, to keep GM crops out of virtually all of Africa, as documented by Robert Paarlberg in his powerful (and to some, infuriating) book *Starved For Science*.

I have absolutely no doubt that the opponents of genetically modified foods, and particularly those campaigning against their planting in the developing world, are doing this with the best of intentions. They fully believe that they're protecting people in Africa, India, the Philippines, and elsewhere against poisons, against corporate control of their food, or against destruction of their environment. Yet I wish more of them would read Nathanael Johnson's carefully thought-out series here and in particular his argument that most of the debate is highly inflamed.

Most of the perceived ills of genetically modified foods are either illusory or far smaller than believed. And what the data suggests is that the benefits, while modest in the rich world today, might be quite substantial in the future, and are already much larger in the parts of the world where the battle over GMO approval is most actively raging.

GMOs are neither poison nor panacea. What they are is a toolkit, a varied one, with real benefits to the environment and millions of people today; with the real potential to have a larger positive impact *immediately* if they're allowed to; and with the possibility of a dramatically larger benefit down the road as the science behind them improves.

> *"For some people, the possibility of a risk is enough to make that decision to stop eating GMOs."*

We Need to Err on the Side of Caution

Melis Ann

In the following viewpoint, Melis Ann takes on the question of the health risks of genetically modified foods. While admitting that we still don't know about the safety or long-term effects of GM foods, the author cites studies and anecdotal evidence indicating that there may be more risk than we've so far discovered. In that case, she argues, we should err on the side of caution and avoid GM foods. Melis Ann is an environmental scientist and mother.

As you read, consider the following questions:

1. How, according to the author, do the United States and Europe differ in their approaches to evaluating the safety of new food and medical products?
2. The author opens with the claim that "by the time you're done reading this article, you will be fuming." Does the article have that effect on you? Why or why not?
3. Who did the White House hire to spearhead biotechnology programs, according to the viewpoint? Why might that choice have been problematic?

By the time you're done reading this article, you will be fuming. There is scientific data that shows that GMOs have dangerous side effects in animals. There is evidence, based on animal studies, that eating genetically modified foods causes a wide variety of problems, which makes tracing the source of the problem difficult, especially over time. There is not enough data to show the long-term effects of eating food that has been genetically altered, but some scientists predict that GMOs are one of the root causes of epidemics that now plague the United States including obesity, diabetes, asthma, fertility problems, food allergies, and even cancer. What about ADHD and autism? There are many conditions that are on the rise which coincide with the introduction of changes in our food system over time.

According to the Academy of Environmental Medicine, there should be "an immediate moratorium on genetically modified foods."

What Is Genetically Modified Food?

Confusion exists over the difference between genetically modified crops and hybrid crops. A hybrid is a cross between two plant varieties. The goal with a hybrid crop is to produce a plant that has the best features of each of the crossed varieties. This is done in controlled ways but also can happen in nature.

Genetic engineering of crops involves altering the genetic makeup of a crop in some way, typically for the purpose of making that crop perform better. DNA is extracted from animals, viruses, bacteria, insects, and even humans and then inserted into the DNA of the crop.

An example: The pesticide Bt (Bacillus thuringeiensis), a bacterium naturally occurring in soil, is inserted into corn DNA. The pesticide Bt produces a toxin that destroys the intestinal lining in insects upon eating the corn plant. Although this toxin occurs naturally, it would never become part of corn DNA without intervention.

These terms are commonly used to represent food that has been altered genetically.

- Genetically Modified Organism (GMO)
- Genetically Engineered (GE) Food
- Genetically Modified (GM) Food

GMO Controversy

Supporters say GMOs will help solve world hunger by providing more efficient crops that can grow in less ideal climates or soils for example. The FDA reports that there is no evidence that GMOs are harmful to us and that these crops are held to the same safety standards as non-GMO foods. Big companies that benefit from selling GMO products, like Monsanto, oppose labeling GMOs on food products and maintain that they are perfectly safe for consumers to eat.

Those against GMOs site their own scientific research that says GMOs cause allergies, infertility, reproductive problems, organ damage, insulin regulation problems, accelerated aging, immune problems, and changes to the gastrointestinal system. Many organizations and scientists agree that there is not enough data about the long-term side effects of ingesting GMOs.

Which Foods Are Genetically Modified?

Some examples of foods that are genetically modified:

- 93% of soybean fields in the United States are genetically modified and 77% worldwide.
- 85% of corn in the United States is genetically modified and 26% worldwide, affecting products that contain canola oil, corn syrup, cornmeal, xanthan gum, and cornstarch.
- 95% of sugar beet crops grown in the US in 2010 were genetically engineered and 9% worldwide.
- 93% of cotton is modified, 49% worldwide affecting cottonseed oil.
- 80% of Hawaiian papaya is genetically altered.

- 70-90% of processed foods on grocery store shelves contain GM foods.
- livestock is fed GM foods, affecting meat, milk, and eggs.

What Do Scientists Say About GMOs?

Scientists have been harassed, fired, and received death threats for publishing information or expressing opinions such as the following against GMOs.

- Scientists speculate that the rise in infertility, low birth weight babies and other reproductive ailments in the US population since the mid-1990s may be linked to the introduction of genetically modified foods.
- The American Academy of Environmental Medicine asked doctors to educate patients about the dangerous effects of eating GM foods.
- Scientists at the FDA warned the White House in the 1990s that potential side effects of GMO foods would be difficult to detect. Instead of gathering more long-term data, the White House appointed Monsanto's former attorney to push the US forward with GMOs and biotechnology. FYI: Monsanto sells approximately 90% of the genetically modified seeds used in the United States. Many of these seeds are modified to give the crops the ability to withstand heavy doses of the herbicide Roundup, also a Monsanto product.
- Dr. Pushpa M. Bhargave, a biologist known around the world, believes that the increase in diseases and disorders that are affecting Americans today are due to GMOs. His opinions are based on a review of 600 scientific documents and journals about GMOs.
- The global scientific community continues to express that there is not enough data to show that GMOs are safe for humans. More testing and understanding is needed. They state that we have all become guinea pigs in a huge scientific experiment.

- Other scientists point out that because the effects of eating GMOs are not understood, new diseases are likely to develop without us knowing exactly why until too much time has passed. An example of this already occurred in the 1980s when a genetically engineered food supplement called L-tryptophan killed people and caused illness and disability because it took four years to find the cause.
- It is reported that more and more doctors are prescribing GM-free diets.
- The American approach to food safety is based on "substantial equivalence" whereas the European approach is based on "precautionary principle." The FDA says there isn't evidence to support that GMOs are not safe; European officials say that if a reasonable risk exists it is not worth continuing to eat GMOs. This situation is repeated with other food safety issues, like the use of food dyes.

Allergies from Genetically Modified Food

Genetically modified soy contains up to seven times more of the allergen called trypsin inhibitor than non-GM soy. It is reported that soy allergies increased 50% around the same time that genetically modified soy began being used in the UK. Many of these individuals react to skin prick tests for GM soy, but don't have evidence of an allergy to the non-GM soy.

Side Effects of GMOs

Since we don't know exactly what GMOs do to our health, we have to base our decision to eat GMOs on evidence from animal studies and the opinions of experts in the scientific field. For some people, the possibility of a risk is enough to make that decision to stop eating GMOs.

See the table below for some specific findings related to GMO studies, including a human study showing that DNA from the modified food inserts itself into bacteria present in human intestines.

Studies on GMO Foods

FOOD SOURCE	EXPERIMENT	EFFECTS OF GMOS IN DIET
genetically modified foods	fed to rats and salmon	increased weight gain, ate more, changes in immune system, altered intestinal structure http://sciencenordic.com/growing-fatter-gm-diet
genetically modified soy	humans (the only published human study)	the gene inserted into GM soy transfers into the DNA of bacteria living in human intestines—the gene now functions within the bacteria
genetically modified soy	fed to mice	embryos developed significant DNA changes
genetically modified soy	fed to hamsters over 3 generations	3rd generation lost ability to have babies, high mortality of offspring, slower growth, some had hair growing inside mouths
genetically modified soybeans or corn	fed to mice and rats; combination of 19 studies	significant organ disruption; livers and kidneys
genetically engineered soy	tested goats milk	found the modified DNA sequences in the goats milk, having passed from the intestines to the blood stream to the udders into the milk
genetically engineered plants	analyzed genes in fish	found modified DNA in nearly all inner organs
genetically modified soy	Fed to female rats	most of their babies died within three weeks, babies were smaller, offspring less fertility
genetically modified corn	fed to mice	fewer babies, smaller babies
genetially modified cottonseed	fed to buffalo in India	premature deliveries, abortions, infertility, prolapsed uteruses
genetically modified corn	fed to pigs in US	became sterile, had false pregnancies, gave birth to bags of water
genetically modified corn	fed to cows and bulls	became infertile
multiple genetically altered foods	various animals	significant immune dysregulaton - associated with asthma, allergy and inflammation

GMOs Are High Risk

Based on this extensive list of animal studies that show severe side effects, GMOs appear to be a risky addition to the food supply. More data need to be gathered, but not at the expense of our health.

> *"Several cancer rates in the US are rising in parallel with increased use of glyphosate on GMO soy and corn fields."*

GMO Products May Cause Cancer

Jeffrey Smith

The following viewpoint is from the website of the Institute for Responsible Technology, an organization operated by Jeffrey Smith, to educate the public about the dangers of GMO foods and advocate for labelling of GMO foods. Here, Smith specifically addresses the question of whether GMOs (and the herbicide Roundup, in particular) cause cancer. Jeffrey Smith is a consumer activist, author, and the executive director of the Institute for Responsible Technology.

As you read, consider the following questions:

1. What is the product Roundup (glyphosate) used for, according to this viewpoint?
2. Why is avoiding non-GMO products not enough to eliminate exposure to Roundup? What solution does the author suggest?
3. In the study cited near the end of the viewpoint, how are the effects of switching to non-GMO foods determined?

"GMOs and Cancer," by Jeffrey Smith, The Institute for Responsible Technology. Reprinted by permission.

Here are GMOs and Roundup linked to cancer? That was the subject of my talk in Orlando at the exciting The Truth About Cancer conference. Here are 10 main points from my presentation:

1. The very process of creating a GMO creates side effects that can promote cancer. Monsanto's Roundup Ready corn, for example, has higher levels of putrescine and cadaverine. These are not only linked to cancer and allergies, they produce the foul smell of rotting dead bodies.

2. Bt-toxin, which is manufactured by the altered DNA in every cell of genetically modified varieties of corn, cotton, and South American soy, pokes holes in cell walls. It may create "leaky gut," which is linked to cancer and numerous other diseases.

3. Most GMOs are "Roundup Ready"—designed to be sprayed with Monsanto's Roundup herbicide. These include Soy, Corn, Cotton, Canola, Sugar Beets (for sugar), and Alfalfa. Glyphosate, the active ingredient in Roundup, is classified as a class 2A carcinogen by the International Agency for Research on Cancer (part of the World Health Organization). They said it probably causes cancer in humans, does cause cancer in animals, does cause mutations in DNA that can lead to cancer, and where it is heavily sprayed, cancer rates are higher.

4. Roundup is also sprayed on numerous non-GMO crops just before harvest as a desiccant, to dry down the crop as it is killed by the herbicide. Some of these other crops include: Wheat, Oats, Flax, Peas, Lentils, Dry Beans, Sugar Cane, Rye, Triticale, Buckwheat, Millet, Potatoes and Sunflowers. Canola, Corn and Soybeans labeled non-GMO may also be sprayed with Roundup.

5. To avoid Roundup, eating non-GMO is not sufficient. It is better to choose organic, which does not allow the use of GMOs, Roundup, or other synthetic poisons. (Products

GMOs Can Prevent Cancer

Despite the debated pros and cons to genetically altering food, there are some intriguing, if sometimes bizzare, new uses of GMO science to help humanity. Scientists have been creating foods that do amazing things, like prevent cancer or deliver antibiotics. Here are some of the more interesting creations from the last few years:

Disease-fighting eggs: In 2007, British scientists inserted two new genes into a breed of chicken known as ISA Brown (this breed has already been genetically selected to have the best egg layers). These new genes caused the chickens to lay eggs with proteins that are able to treat diseases as diverse as skin cancer, arthritis and multiple sclerosis. The protein is found in the egg white of the genetically modified eggs.

Venomous cabbage: Tasked with finding a way to combat the caterpillars who eat cabbage in the fields, Chinese scientists inserted a gene into the cabbage that coded for the production of a modified version of scorpion venom. While not toxic to humans, the venom keeps caterpillars at bay and allows farmers to avoid using pesticides.

labeled both Organic and Non-GMO Project Verified are even better, because the latter requires tests for possible inadvertent GMO contamination.) Since Roundup is sprayed on most US cotton, residues are found in cotton products including tampons. BUY ORGANIC!

6. Several cancer rates in the US are rising in parallel with increased use of glyphosate on GMO soy and corn fields. These include leukemia and cancers of the liver, kidney, bladder, thyroid, and breast.

7. In Argentina, the rate of cancer in communities living near Roundup Ready soybean fields has also skyrocketed, as have birth defects, thyroid conditions, lupus, and respiratory problems.

Vaccine in a banana: An altered form of a virus is inserted into the banana sapling so that the virus' genetic material becomes a permanent part of the plant's cells. The plant will then produce the virus proteins but not the infectious parts of the virus. When people eat the banana and ingest these proteins, their immune systems respond by building up immunity to the disease, in the same way that traditional vaccines work but without the shot and in an easily transportable container.

Plants that capture carbon: In our efforts to stem the release of carbon into the atmosphere, some scientists have turned to genetically modifying plants and trees so that they become capable of capturing and storing carbon from the atmosphere. The plants are engineered to store more carbon than usual in their root systems.

Whether you believe genetic alteration of plants and animals is a good or bad thing, the reality is its happening all over the world in many different ways. Certain forms of GMO organisms may serve to help solve some of our biggest issues and some may serve to cause more problems than they fix. The future remains quite open on this complex issue, so stay tuned.

"GMOs That Prevent Cancer," by Aubrey Yee, Sustainable America, July 17, 2012.

8. The following are just some of the health effects of glyphosate, all of which are known to increase cancer risk. Glyphosate:

   1. Damages the DNA

   2. Is an antibiotic

   3. Promotes leaky gut

   4. Chelates minerals, making them unavailable

   5. Is toxic to the mitochondria

   6. Interferes with key metabolic pathways

   7. Causes non-alcoholic fatty liver disease

   8. Degrades into Sarcosine and formaldehyde

9. The full Roundup formulation is up to 125 times more toxic than glyphosate alone. It also has a greater endocrine disruptive effect.

10. Thousands of people who were exposed to Roundup and are now suffering from non-Hodgkin's lymphoma are suing Monsanto. The lawsuit forced Monsanto to make public secret documents, emails, and texts. These are smoking guns, providing clear evidence that Monsanto colludes with government regulators, bullies scientists, ghostwrites articles, pays off journal editors and scientists, and publicly denies evidence of harm that it privately admits to.

I ended my talk by introducing a peer-reviewed article that was recently accepted for publication. It features survey results in which 3,256 people describe significant improvements in 28 conditions after switching to non-GMO (and often organic) food. Of the 155 people who reported improvement in cancer after making the change, 23% said there was "Significant improvement," 17% said the condition was "Nearly gone," and 42% had a "Complete Recovery."

My new film *Secret Ingredients*, created with Amy Hart, has an excellent section on cancer. Information on the film and the new peer reviewed article are coming soon.

*"Overregulation has become a real
threat to the development and use
of GM crops. Zero regulation is not
desirable, either."*

We Need a Better Approach to Regulating Genetically Modified Crops

Matin Qaim

*Previous authors have argued that because there are so many
unanswered questions about the safety of genetically modified foods,
these products should be regulated and labeled. In the following
viewpoint, the author acknowledges some unknowns but points out
that the advantages of GMOs are reduced because of the excessive
regulatory burden on these crops. He offers a solution, however.
Matin Qaim is a professor of international food economics and rural
development at Georg-August-University of Goettingen in Germany.*

"The Benefits of Genetically Modified Crops—and the Costs of Inefficient Regulation," by
Matin Qaim, Resources for the Future (RFF), April 2, 2010. Reprinted by permission.

As you read, consider the following questions:

1. Why, according to Qaim's explanation, is it possible to use genetic engineering to alter the traits of an organism in ways that traditional breeding could not have done?
2. What are some of the benefits of GMOs mentioned in this viewpoint?
3. What solution does the author offer to the problem of overly complex regulation of GM crops?

Plant genetic engineering methods were developed over 30 years ago, and since then, genetically modified (GM) crops have become commercially available and widely adopted. In 2009, GM crops were being grown on 10 percent of the Earth's arable land.

In these plants, one or more genes coding for desirable traits have been inserted. The genes may come from the same or another plant species, or from totally unrelated organisms. The traits targeted through genetic engineering are often the same as those pursued by conventional breeding. However, because genetic engineering allows for direct gene transfer across species boundaries, some traits that were previously difficult or impossible to breed can now be developed with relative ease.

So-called first-generation GM crops have improved traits. Herbicide-resistant soybeans and corn (maize), for example, can be "weeded" with herbicides that are more effective, less toxic, and cheaper than the alternatives. Cotton and corn have been modified to incorporate Bacillus thuringiensis (Bt) genes, producing proteins that are toxic only to larval pests. Crops can also be modified to ward off plant viruses or fungi. Even though the seed is more expensive, these GM crops lower the costs of production by reducing inputs of machinery, fuel, and chemical pesticides. In addition, due to more effective pest control, crop yields are often higher.

Important environmental benefits, such as controlling farm runoff that otherwise pollutes water systems, are associated with reduced spraying of chemical insecticides and highly toxic herbicides. Reduced mechanical weeding helps prevent the loss of topsoil. Health benefits result from reduced pesticide exposure for farmers and rural laborers and lower pesticide residues for consumers.

Where Bt crops have been grown in developing countries, the technology appears to often generate employment, because more workers are needed to harvest the significantly higher yields. One study in India suggests that Bt cotton produces 82 percent higher incomes for small-farm households compared with conventional cotton—a remarkable gain in overall economic welfare.

Recent research shows that direct and indirect effects of Bt cotton increase aggregate welfare by over $2 billion per year in India alone; a significant share of these gains go to rural households living below the poverty line. The annual gains of Bt cotton in China are also estimated in a range of $1 billion. Other developing countries where farmers use Bt cotton include Pakistan, South Africa, Burkina Faso, Mexico, and Argentina.

GM soybeans and corn, which are widely grown in North and South America as well as South Africa and a few other countries, also produce large aggregate welfare gains, currently estimated at $5 billion per year at the global level. Huge benefits are also projected for future GM crops that are more tolerant to drought or more efficient in nutrient use.

In terms of the distribution of benefits, interesting differences can be observed between developed and developing countries. In developed countries, where GM technologies are mostly patented, large profits accrue to biotech and seed companies. In contrast, intellectual property protection is relatively weak in most developing countries, so that GM seed prices are lower and farmers' benefit shares higher. For example, soybean farmers in Argentina or cotton farmers in China and India capture over 70 percent of the overall GM technology benefits. Consumers benefit, too, because new technologies tend to lower the price of food and other agricultural products.

Second-generation GM crops involve enhanced quality traits, such as higher nutrient content. "Golden Rice," one of the very first GM crops, is biofortified to address vitamin A deficiency, a common condition in developing countries that leads to blindness and entails higher rates of child mortality and infectious diseases. Other biofortification projects include corn, sorghum, cassava, and banana plants, with enhanced minerals and vitamins. Widespread production and consumption of biofortified staple crops could improve health outcomes and provide economic benefits in a very cost-effective way, especially in rural areas of developing countries. A recent simulation shows that Golden Rice could reduce health problems associated with vitamin A deficiency by up to 60 percent in rice-eating populations.

Regulation of GM Crops

Despite all those real and potential advantages, GM crops have aroused significant opposition, particularly in Europe. The major concerns relate to potential environmental and health risks, such as allergenicity of transgenes or loss of biodiversity. But there are also fears about adverse social implications—for instance, that GM technology could undermine traditional knowledge systems in developing countries—and the monopolization of seed markets and exploitation of small farmers.

Unexpected risks have not materialized so far, and those risks that do exist seem to be manageable. There is even evidence that GM technology can contribute to the preservation of agrobiodiversity, because the new traits can be inserted into local heirloom varieties. Nevertheless, concerns have led to complex and costly biosafety, food safety, and labeling regulations.

Governments have responsibility for ensuring that foods are safe for consumption and that new agricultural inputs do not damage the environment or harm agricultural production. Most countries require GM products be approved before they may be grown, consumed, or imported. Because approval processes are not internationally harmonized, they have become a major barrier to the spread of GM crops and technologies. For example, the European Union has not yet approved some of the GM corn technologies used in the United States and Argentina, which obstructs trade not only in technologies but also in commodity and food markets.

Often, the regulators are extremely cautious and require extended regulatory trials over many years. The arduous testing comes at a cost: one estimate puts private compliance costs for approval of a new Bt corn technology in just one country at $6 million to $15 million. Beyond the direct regulatory costs are the indirect costs of forgone benefits—preventing the use of safe products.

Such high regulatory costs slow down overall innovation rates. They also impede the commercialization of GM technologies in minor crops and small countries, where markets are not large enough to justify the fixed-cost investments. Expensive regulations discourage small firms, thereby contributing to the further concentration of the agricultural biotech industry.

Reforming Policy

The regulatory complexity appears to be the outcome of the politicized debate and lobbying success of antibiotech interest groups, especially in Europe. Even though genetic engineering does not entail unique risks, GM crops are subjected to a much higher degree of scrutiny than conventionally bred crops. Some reform of GM regulations will be necessary, and economists have an important role in quantifying the costs and benefits.

A "safety rule" approach could be useful here. It combines a probabilistic risk assessment model with a safety rule decision mechanism and can be employed for cost-benefit and risk-benefit analyses. Its transparent criteria would bring science and objectivity to decision-making processes that are often influenced by political economy considerations and a precautionary approach.

Overregulation has become a real threat to the development and use of GM crops. Zero regulation is not desirable, either, but the trade-offs associated with regulation—particularly the forgone benefits for developing countries—should be considered. In the public arena, the risks of GM crops seem to be overrated, while the benefits are underrated.

> *"GMOs are more thoroughly tested than any product produced in the history of agriculture."*

Commercially Available GMOs Are Safe to Eat

Editors of Best Food Facts

We close out this chapter with a viewpoint that includes the perspectives of several experts. The editors of the website Best Food Facts asked four experts from a variety of universities about the health risks of eating GM foods. Though their answers reflect the complexity of the issue, they are somewhat reassuring. Best Food Facts is a website that provides consumers with scientific information about food. The experts' affiliations are listed in the viewpoint.

As you read, consider the following questions:

1. How, according to Newell-McGloughlin, might GMO foods actually reduce the incidence of allergies?
2. What examples does Lemaux give of foods that have been made more nutritious by genetic engineering?
3. What counterargument does Parrott make to the claim that US regulatory agencies can't be trusted? Does this seem satisfying to you? Why or why not?

G MOs—we've read about them in the news, have researched their ancient roots and continue to have discussions with our family and friends about them. GMOs, genetically modified organisms, or even "frankenfood," as they have been called have been eaten by consumers for many years.

What are the health risks of eating GMO foods? Are GMO foods less nutritious? Do they cause allergies? What foods are GMOs? To address our reader's concerns, we put these questions before a panel of experts:

- Peggy Lemaux, Cooperative Extension Specialist at the University of California—Berkeley
- Wayne Parrott, Professor in the Department of Crop and Soil Sciences College of Agricultural & Environmental Sciences University of Georgia, University of Georgia
- Bruce Chassy, Professor of Food Microbiology and Nutritional Sciences; Executive Associate Director of the Biotechnology Center; Assistant Dean for Science Communications in the College of Agricultural, Consumer and Environmental Sciences, University of Illinois—Urbana/Champaign
- Martina Newell-McGloughlin, Director, University of California Systemwide Biotechnology Research and Education Program (UCBREP), Co-Director, National Institutes of Health Training Program in Biomolecular Technology, Co-Director, NSF IGERT CREATE Training Program, and Adjunct Associate Professor, Department of Plant Pathology at the University of California-Davis.

Are GMO fruits and vegetables less nutritious than non-GMO or organic fruits and vegetables?

Dr. Lemaux: "That's a good question! Foods that have been genetically modified undergo testing for safety, health and nutrient value. The nutritional value of GMO foods is tested and compared against non-GMO foods. Numerous studies have shown no nutritional differences between commercially available GMO and non-GMO foods. In fact, genetic modification can improve the nutritional content of some foods, for example, low linoleic acid canola oil that can reduce trans-fat content. In these cases, the foods must be labeled to show the nutritional differences according to FDA policy."

Dr. Parrott: "Before any GMO can come to market, it must undergo extensive testing to ensure that the content of vitamins, minerals and other nutrients is not inadvertently altered during the final process. For every study that finds nutritional superiority in organic produce, another finds it in GMO produce. The bottom line is to make sure you eat as many fresh fruits and vegetables as you can, regardless of whether they are organic or GMO."

Dr. Chassy: "Recent reviews have concluded that there is no difference in nutrient quality between organic and non-organic produce. Some disagree because they believe (not based on science, but rather, personal beliefs) that organic matter derived from living organisms provides a vital life force to crops that cannot be supplied by inorganic chemical fertilizers. This is just not the case when we look at this based on research. This thinking has transitioned into a belief by some that organic is more nutritious, which has simply not been proven."

Do GMOs cause allergies?

Dr. Lemaux: "GM foods that are in the grocery stores (commercially available) are not likely to cause allergic reactions any more so than non-GM foods. Food allergies are nothing new, and under the FDA's biotechnology food policy, GMO foods must be labeled as such if the genetic information comes from one of the eight most common allergy-causing foods, unless the new food is shown to be allergy-free. Those foods are dairy, eggs, fish, shellfish, tree nuts, wheat, soybeans, and peanuts. All GMO foods undergo food safety testing that focuses on the source of the gene or protein product that has been introduced into the food. Even so, no food product can be deemed 100% safe, whether it be conventional (non-GMO), GMO or organic. For example, peanuts can cause severe allergies regardless of how they're grown—so they would be considered unsafe for some people."

Dr. Chassy: "Food allergies dramatically change the lives of people who have them. Fortunately, only a very small percentage of people are allergic to any one food. This is because food allergy is almost always caused by specific proteins present in the offending food, but the great majority of proteins (>99.9999+%) that we consume do not cause allergies. It is important to stress that there is no a prior reason to believe that GM foods might cause allergies, and to date, none has."

Dr. Newell-McGloughlin: "No. In fact, the work that is being done in GMO research can, in fact, reduce allergies. There are very specific sets of indicators that determine whether a specific protein in GMOs would cause an allergic response. Those proteins that are difficult to digest cause an allergic response, causing the body to create antibodies to them. This can happen with a number of proteins, but there is nothing inherent about biotech products that would cause allergies."

Are there health risks associated with consuming GMOs?

Dr. Newell-McGloughlin: "No. GMOs are more thoroughly tested than any product produced in the history of agriculture. We use many methods to introduce desired traits—to try to get specific characteristics into our crops. With GMOs, they are thoroughly tested before any product is released into the marketplace. In all the risk assessments in over 15 years of field research and 30 years of laboratory research, there hasn't been a single instance where there was a health risk associated with a GMO product."

Some believe that the FDA's research
on GMOs' impacts on health is flawed.
What are your thoughts on that?

Dr. Newell-McGloughlin: "In the US, GMOs are more highly regulated than any other methods to introduce traits into crops today, by three different agencies:

- Food and Drug Administration
- United States Department of Agriculture: Animal and Plant Health Inspection Service (APHIS)
- Environmental Protection Agency

The primary body that regulates the commercialization of GMOs is USDA-APHIS. This is a lengthy process which, for most regulation, takes several years to determine whether approval will be granted. No other product or system that is used to introduce desired traits undergoes the same level of scrutiny as do the products of modern biotechnology."

Dr. Parrott: "Although there is no indication that the FDA has made a wrong call on any GM product, the point remains that we are in a global economy. Thus, it is not just FDA who approves these foods, but also FoodCanada, the European Food Safety Authority, the Food Standards for Australia and New Zealand, and various agencies in Japan and Korea, among others. It is one thing to say that FDA's procedures might be flawed; it is another to say every major food safety agency is flawed. Thus far, I am not aware of any situation whereby one agency gave a GM product a clean bill of health and another failed to do so."

Dr. Chassy: "There was never any scientific reason to believe that foods produced using biotechnology present any new, different or special hazards. From a scientific perspective, they pose even fewer hazards than the conventionally bred crops that we have been eating safely for millennia. The pre-market regulatory review is intended to ensure the consumer that GM foods have been checked for safety before they go to market. In the heat of the argument, we often lose sight of the fact that every expert analysis of the safety of GM crops has concluded that they are as safe as any other crop."

In summary, GMO foods are just as safe to consume as conventional, organic, or non-GMO foods.

Periodical and Internet Sources Bibliography

The following articles have been selected to supplement the diverse views presented in this chapter.

Jennifer Ackerman, "Food: How Altered," *National Geographic*, May 2002.

Dominique Bonessi, "GMO Foods Pose Greater Risk to Agriculture than Human Health, Experts Say," PBS *NewsHour,* 17 May 2016. https://www.pbs.org/newshour/nation/gmo-foods-pose-greater-risk-to-agriculture-than-human-health-experts-say

Jane E. Brody, "Are G.M.O. Foods Safe?" *The New York Times,* 23 April 2018. https://www.nytimes.com/2018/04/23/well/eat/are-gmo-foods-safe.html

Rene Ebersole, "Did Monsanto Ignore Evidence Linking Its Weed Killer to Cancer?" *Nation*, 12 October 2017. https://www.thenation.com/article/did-monsanto-ignore-evidence-linking-its-weed-killer-to-cancer/

David H. Freedman, "The Truth about Genetically Modified Food," *Scientific American*, 1 September 2013. https://www.scientificamerican.com/article/the-truth-about-genetically-modified-food/

Erik Kobayashi-Solomon, "Here's the Real Reason Why GMOs Are Bad, and Why they May Save Humanity," *Forbes*, 15 February 2019. https://www.forbes.com/sites/erikkobayashisolomon/2019/02/15/heres-the-real-reason-why-gmos-are-bad-and-why-they-may-save-humanity/#2617aa464877

Mark Lallanilla, "What Are GMOs and GMO Foods?" *LiveScience*, 8 July 2019. https://www.livescience.com/40895-gmo-facts.html

Lauren Mazzo, "Are There Possible Health Risks to GMO Foods?" *Shape*, 8 November 2017. https://www.shape.com/healthy-eating/diet-tips/possible-health-risks-gmos-gmo-foods

Megan L. Norris, "Will GMOs Hurt My Body? The Public's Concerns and How Scientists Have Addressed Them," Science in the News, Harvard University Graduate School of Arts and Sciences, 10 August 2015. http://sitn.hms.harvard.edu/flash/2015/will-gmos-hurt-my-body/

William Reville, "Are Genetically Modified Organisms Safe?" *Irish Times*, 2 August 2018. https://www.irishtimes.com/news/science/are-genetically-modified-organisms-safe-1.3575044

William Saletan, "Unhealthy Fixation," Slate, 15 July 2015. http://www.slate.com/articles/health_and_science/science/2015/07/are_gmos_safe_yes_the_case_against_them_is_full_of_fraud_lies_and_errors.html

Stuart Smyth, "25 Years of GMO Crops: Economic, Environmental, and Human Health Benefits," Genetic Literacy Project, 6 April 2018. https://geneticliteracyproject.org/2018/04/06/25-years-of-gmo-crops-economic-environmental-and-human-health-benefits/

Elizabeth Weise, "Academies of Science Finds GMOs Not Harmful to Human Health," *USA Today*, 17 May 2016, https://www.usatoday.com/story/tech/2016/05/17/gmos-safe-academies-of-science-report-genetically-modified-food/84458872/

OPPOSING
VIEWPOINTS®
SERIES

CHAPTER 2

Do Genetically Modified Crops Pose a Danger to the Environment?

Chapter Preface

The issue of human health and the health of the environment are impossible to untangle. Nonetheless, the viewpoints in this chapter, by and large, focus less on human health than on the health of the ecosystem of which humans are a part. One of the deepest concerns about GMOs and one of the areas with many still unanswered questions is how GMOs will affect the balance of nature and, ultimately, humans' ability to survive on planet Earth.

Climate change has further complicated the issue. A rapidly warming planet is affecting ecosystems and food production. As you will see in this chapter, some GMO advocates believe that GMOs can help, if not solve entirely, problems posed by global warming. Others believe that GMOs will merely accelerate the environmental apocalypse. One of the reasons it is so difficult to assess the potential damage of GMOs on human health is that so many intermingling factors have to be taken into account. The same is the case—perhaps even more so—with the environment.

In this chapter you will read viewpoints that sound the alarm about GMOs getting loose in the environment and breeding with wild plants. You will read about GMOs that are so well adapted for a given environment that they out-compete native plants and thus reduce diversity. And you will read one viewpoint that argues that rather than using technology to solve Earth's problems, we should opt for a very low-tech approach to saving the environment and feeding the world.

The closing viewpoint is an interesting take on the issue from the turn of the twenty-first century, when the issue of GMOs was still new and tantalizing. However, as you will see, even then the technology already posed a variety of questions and potential complications, not all having to do with health, whether it be human or environmental.

> *"The finding provides, however, a warning for future genetic modifications that might increase fitness in all kinds of plants; it will be difficult to keep those traits on the farm and out of the wild."*

A Genetically Modified Crop Is Loose and Evolving

David Biello

In the following viewpoint, David Biello reports on a disturbing development in the introduction of genetically altered plants. Transgenic canola plants have been found growing in the wild. The viewpoint raises questions—but offers no answers—to the potential problems of releasing genetically altered organisms into the environment. David Biello is an environmental journalist, science curator for TED, and contributing editor at Scientific American.

"Genetically Modified Crop on the Loose and Evolving in US Midwest," by David Biello, Scientific American, August 6, 2010. Reprinted by permission.

As you read, consider the following questions:

1. What was the significance of the transgenic canola the researchers found growing wild in North Dakota?
2. Why is the potential of the new genes to either increase or decrease fitness an important consideration?
3. Biello says that this development will be useful in helping scientists learn how these genes might move through a population. Why might that be important?

Outside a grocery store in Langdon, N.D., two ecologists spotted a yellow canola plant growing on the margins of a parking lot this summer. They plucked it, ground it up and, using a chemical stick similar to those in home pregnancy kits, identified proteins that were made by artificially introduced genes. The plant was GM—genetically modified.

That's not too surprising, given that North Dakota grows tens of thousands of hectares of conventional and genetically modified canola—a weedy plant, known scientifically as Brassica napus var oleifera, bred by Canadians to yield vegetable oil from its thousands of tiny seeds. What was more surprising was that nearly everywhere the two ecologists and their colleagues stopped during a trip across the state, they found GM canola growing in the wild. "We found transgenic plants growing in the middle of nowhere, far from fields," says ecologist Cindy Sagers of the University of Arkansas (U.A.) in Fayetteville, who presented the findings August 6 at the Ecological Society of America meeting in Pittsburgh. Most intriguingly, two of the 288 tested plants showed man-made genes for resistance to multiple pesticides—so-called "stacked traits," and a type of seed that biotechnology companies like Monsanto have long sought to develop and market. As it seems, Mother Nature beat biotech to it. "One of the ones with multiple traits was [in the middle of] nowhere, and believe me, there's a lot of nowhere in North Dakota—nowhere near a canola field," she adds.

That likely means that transgenic canola plants are cross-pollinating in the wild—and swapping introduced genes. Although GM canola in the wild has been identified everywhere from Canada to Japan in previous research, this marks the first time such plants have been shown to be evolving in this way. "They had novel combinations of transgenic traits," Sagers says. "The most parsimonious explanation is these traits are stable outside of cultivation and they are evolving."

Escaped populations of such transgenic plants have generally died out quickly without continual replenishment from stray farm seeds in places such as Canada, but canola is capable of hybridizing with at least two—and possibly as many as eight—wild weed species in North America, including field mustard (Brassica rapa), which is a known agricultural pest. "Not only is it going to jump out of cultivation; there are sexually compatible weeds all over North America," Sagers says. Adds ecologist-in-training Meredith Schafer of U.A., who led the research, "It becomes a weed [farmers] can't control."

There has been no evidence to show that the herbicide resistance genes will either increase or decrease fitness to date. The finding provides, however, a warning for future genetic modifications that might increase fitness in all kinds of plants; it will be difficult to keep those traits on the farm and out of the wild. "The big concern is traits that would increase invasiveness or weediness, traits such as drought tolerance, salt tolerance, heat or cold tolerance" says weed scientist Carol Mallory-Smith of Oregon State University—all the traits that Monsanto and others are currently developing to help crops adapt to climate change. "These traits would have the possibility of expanding a species' range." In the case of canola, consider it done—at least in North Dakota.

This is not the first transgenic crop to escape into the wild in the US; herbicide-resistant turf grass being tested in Oregon spread as well in 2006. And GM canola is not a regulated plant, "therefore no protocols are required by the regulatory agencies to reduce or prevent escape," notes ecologist Allison Snow of The Ohio State

University. "The next question is: 'So what?' What difference does it make if the feral canola or any species that hybridize with it have two transgenes for herbicide resistance?"

Canola modified to resist either the herbicide glufosinate (brand name Liberty) or glyphosate (brand name Roundup) has been available in the US since 1989—and unregulated since 1998 and 1999, respectively for the two herbicides. "These results are not new for Canadian researchers and to be expected if two types of transgenic herbicide-resistant canola are commercially grown," says Suzanne Warwick of Agriculture and Agri-Food Canada, a government agency.

A common source for GM canola in the wild is seed that has scattered during harvest or fallen off a truck during transport. "Because about 90 percent of the US and Canadian canola crop is biotech, it is reasonable to expect a survey of roadside canola to show similar levels of biotech plants," said Tom Nickson, environmental policy lead at Monsanto, in a prepared statement.

Nor does Monsanto claim ownership of the escaped plants, even those with multiple transgenes, according to company spokesman John Combest. "It has never been, nor will it be, Monsanto policy to exercise its patent rights where trace amounts of our patented traits are present in fields as a result of inadvertent means," although researchers would have to obtain a license from the company to work with the GM plant.

It remains to be seen how much sexual mingling such transgenic plants do; U.A.'s Sagers plans to do greenhouse trials starting in a few weeks. But it does provide a compelling example of how genes might move through a given population. "This is a good model for the influence of agriculture on the evolution of native plants," she says. "We can imagine gene flow to native species. If we can imagine it happening, it probably happens."

"GE crops are generally beneficial to the environment, given their reduced land usage, need for pesticides, and lack of off-target effects."

GMOs Are Better for the Environment Than You Probably Think

Marco Giovannetti

The previous viewpoint raised issues about potential environmental dangers of GMOs. In the following viewpoint, Marco Giovannetti points out ways in which GMOs might actually be good for the environment. GMO crops can reduce the need for pesticides, Giovannetti argues, and this can actually increase biodiversity. Marco Giovannetti is a plant biologist at the Gregor Mendel Institute in Vienna, Austria.

As you read, consider the following questions:

1. How does the author define sustainability?
2. Why, according to this viewpoint, does farming reduce biodiversity?
3. How might GMOs help reduce the impact of climate change, according to the author?

"GMOs Are Better for the Environment Than You'd Think," by Marco Giovannetti, Massive Science Inc, August 1, 2018. Reprinted by permission.

So Far, GMOs Aren't Helping the Environment

In a recent interview for New York magazine's Grub Street, author and food activist Michael Pollan laid out why he believes that food containing genetically modified ingredients (GMOs) should be labeled — and why GMO crops have been bad for the environment.

"GMOs have been, I think, a tremendous disappointment," Pollan said. "They haven't done what Monsanto promised they would do, which is make American agriculture more sustainable."

Seed and chemical companies like Monsanto claimed that genetically engineered crops would be good for the environment by reducing pesticide use and increasing crop yields, but the past 20 years have shown that they do nothing of the sort. Not only have GMO crops not improved yields, they have vastly increased the use of glyphosate, the active ingredient in Monsanto's Roundup herbicide.

[M]ost GMOs have not been engineered to improve yields or make food healthier, but to be herbicide resistant. Corn, soybeans and other crops have been genetically engineered to withstand blasts of glyphosate. It kills all the weeds in the field, but the GMO crops survive.

Crops are engineered in a number of ways. Often, they are made resistant to an herbicide, so a farmer can spray one on their fields and keep their plots free from weeds without killing the crop itself. Or they can be innately poisonous to its predators, like milkweed is, which reduces the amount of pesticides needed to keep a crop safe.

But do these things harm the environment? According to the data: not really. GM crops appear to be just as sustainable and productive as non-GM crops, if not more so.

"Sustainability," in addition to being a buzzword, is a measure of a local environment's ability to remain diverse and productive. Studies show that choosing to farm either non-GM or GM crops doesn't make much difference when it comes to sustainability. And

Since the introduction of these crops in the mid-1990s, glyphosate use has spread like a cancer across the U.S. Farmers now apply 16 times more of the herbicide than they did before GMOs came on the market. The explosion in glyphosate use is not only bad for farmers' health, it's also bad for the environment, especially for certain birds, insects and other wildlife. For example, populations of monarch butterflies have fallen to all-time lows as the result of massive spraying of glyphosate on crop fields.

University of Minnesota researcher Dr. Karen Oberhauser identified glyphosate as one of the main causes of the depletion of monarchs in the US and Mexico.

At a 2014 press conference in Mexico, Oberhauser said of the butterflies' plight: "Tragically, much of their breeding habitat in this region has been lost to changing agricultural practices, primarily the exploding adoption of genetically modified, herbicide-tolerant crops in the late 20th and early 21st centuries."

Some day, GMO crops may provide real benefits to consumers. So far, however, they have mostly increased the use of glyphosate.

"Are GMOs Bad for the Environment?" by Emily Cassidy, Environmental Working Group, March 9, 2016.

in both aspects, biodiversity and productivity, GM agriculture has been performing better than non-GM crops for the last 20 years.

Biodiversity

Any kind of farming inevitably results in biodiversity loss: the immense diversity of forests and woods is cleared for the monotony and monoculture of the crops we need for our food, feed, fibers, and fuel. And this deforestation and agriculture account for 20-30 percent of all greenhouse gases emissions.

But cultivating GM crops has proven better for biodiversity than the conventional alternative, because one way to maintain biodiversity in a local ecosystem is to reduce pesticide use. A GM crop can do this by carrying its own defenses, making pesticides less necessary. For instance, "Bt" corn is engineered to be toxic to predators that would otherwise prey on it. They don't need as much outside assistance in the form of pesticides sprayed over an entire field.

Another upside to GM crops is that the toxin they carry is specific to their predators, making them less harmful than a spray with collateral effects. That means that primary predators like the European corn borer (nicknamed "the billion dollar bug" because of its heavy effects on the corn market) can be precisely targeted, while leaving other harmless, passerby insects unaffected. Such genetic engineering is remarkably efficient—according to a 2014 meta-analysis, GM-based farming has required 37 percent fewer pesticides than conventional agriculture.

The biodiversity of a field can also be monitored through the levels of insects living on it. A recent meta-study based on 839 publications released over 20 years reaches the conclusion that, worldwide, GM corn does not effect the majority of insect families. Basically, no ladybugs or butterflies were harmed—at least, not more than they would've been through conventional agriculture. The only insects that were affected by the Bt-corn were the European corn borer (the intended target), the Western corn rootworm, and other corn pests.

And, finally, an important aspect of biodiversity is the soil in a given area: one teaspoon of soil contains more living organisms than people in the world and soil microorganisms have a crucial impact on the fertility and the sustainability of agricultural systems. For example, the majority of plant roots establish symbiotic relationships with fungi or bacteria living in the soil that both siphons them nutrients and provides protection against root diseases. Soil microbial communities are not affected by GM crops, which interact with soil microorganisms (worms, insect, fungi, and bacteria) in the same way as non-GM crops.

Productivity

The productivity of GM plants is typically 20 percent higher than that of non-GM ones, making it an appealing way to approach the pressures of the rising global food demand due to population growth. GM crops are also an appealing approach in the face of climate change and pollution.

As climate change progresses, land becomes more arid, usable topsoil is depleted, and water becomes more scarce. Conventional crops are typically not drought tolerant, and so as human-caused climate change continues, agricultural yields could drop. One study found that each degree of warming will result in anywhere from a 3–7 percent drop in global yield in wheat, rice, corn, and soybean. Tactics to adapt to this include engineering crops to retain more water, or adding genes that essentially stabilize cells, make them hardier, and hopefully able to withstand the stresses of a drought.

We have gathered enough data in research performed over 20 years in different parts of the world to show that GE crops are generally beneficial to the environment, given their reduced land usage, need for pesticides, and lack of off-target effects. If we continue to engineer plants for other characteristics (like, say, improved photosynthesis and enhanced plant growth, which would increase yield and reduce land usage further), genetic engineering can be an important ally in protecting the environment and achieving a more sustainable agriculture.

> *"Despite scientists' claims to 'solve' a problem, it is impossible to predict the impacts of even a single gene modification."*

GMOs Pose Several Serious Environmental Concerns

Shirley Martin-Abel

In the following viewpoint, written for a magazine that serves the organic gardening community, Shirley Martin-Abel addresses the issue of genetically modified organisms specifically as they relate to organic gardeners. The author addresses several potential harms from GMOs, including the increased use of pesticides and herbicides, the unknown effects of tinkering with plant genomes, and cross-pollination with non-GMO plants. Shirley Martin-Abel is a horticulturalist and organic gardener.

As you read, consider the following questions:

1. What are "superweeds" and how does the use of glyphosate encourage them, according to the viewpoint?
2. How does the author define "pleiotropy"?
3. What are the dangers of cross-pollination with non-GMO plants in an ecosystem?

Genetic modification is a contentious issue. This article looks particularly at how it is used in crops, and the environmental risks. The issues are complex. But GM is unlikely to go away. As organic growers and suppliers—the more we understand the subject, the greater strength we have in order to influence safety regulations, to prevent contamination, and to encourage governments to support growers and farmers to use other less invasive crop cultivation.

What Is Genetic Modification?

A Genetically Modified Organism (GMO) is one whose genetic material (DNA) has been added to, removed or changed.

Genetic engineering allows scientists to insert desired traits or features into an organism—enhancing a crop's resistance, for instance. This artificial manipulation of DNA would never happen in nature. It replaces the traditional method of selective breeding, a common and completely safe practice used by growers. European law defines a GMO as an organism in which "the genetic material has been altered in a way that does not occur naturally by mating and/or natural recombination."

There are many environmental concerns about GMO crops. We concentrate on just three:

1. Increased Use of Toxic Herbicides and Pesticides

The majority of GM crops are those which have been engineered to be herbicide resistant. "Roundup ready" soya, produced by Monsanto, is grown extensively in North and South America. It allows farmers to spray with a toxic cocktail of glyphosate and other chemicals. This may not harm the crop—but it does create residues and run off, making it disastrous for surrounding ecosystems.

It also encourages the development of "superweeds" which are resistant to glyphosate, such as the giant pig weed, which grows over 2m tall.

Morning Glory is another weed which has developed resistance to glyphosate. This paper (http://phys.org/news/2016-11-shifts-

ADAPTING TO CLIMATE CHANGE

Climate change will place unprecedented pressures on our ability to grow the food we require. These impacts will be particularly severe in developing countries. Scenarios from the International Panel on Climate Change show warming will take place over the next several decades irrespective of any action we take today. The same models show conditions for agriculture will be dramatically different from those which prevail today. Adapting agriculture to these future conditions is essential.

Climate change scientists widely recognize the need for new and improved crop varieties that can withstand these challenges. These improved crops are essential not only to reduce hunger but also to strengthen global food security in the medium and long term. The development of crop varieties that can cope with heat, drought, flood and other weather extremes may well be the single most important step we can take to adapt to climate change. However, breeding new varieties can often take up to 10 years, which mean the dramatically different conditions predicted for 2030 are a mere two breeding cycles away for some crops.

"Crop Diversity: Why it Matters," The Crop Trust.

strategies-herbicide-resistant-superweeds-persist.html) reveals how the plant has evolved a reproductive system which ensures its tolerance of glyphosate. Something not predicted by the genetic engineers. "What kind of evolution are we causing due to impacts that we didn't quite foresee?"questions researchers from the University of Michigan.

Since the introduction of GM, there has been a dramatic increase in the use of glyphosate worldwide.

Proponents of GM argue this is cheaper and simpler weed management for farmers, it reduces tillage (and therefore carbon loss) and that it does not harm the environment or our health (believing glyphosate to be safer than other herbicides).

Critics of GM recognize the terrible damage to the life forms surrounding the crops. The risk to beneficial insects such as pollinators, the residues left in the soil, and the run off into fresh water sources such as rivers and streams. But there is also the potential health risk for humans and animals who consume the crops.

The response, unfortunately, is to create GM crop varieties which are resistant to multiple herbicides, such as Dow's multi-herbicide soybean, engineered to tolerate glyphosate, glufosinate and 2,4-D (an ingredient of the defoliant Agent Orange.) It appears this chemical treadmill benefits GMO seed companies, who also produce the agrichemicals.

2. Pleiotropy

DNA is a complex structure. It is not like Lego—altering it in any way can create new consequences in the cell's composition, as well as its relationship with other cells. Chemists call this Pleiotropy. In every organism, genes, proteins and pathways do not act as isolated units but interact with one another and are regulated in a complex, multi-layered network process. Such is the wonder of natural life.

Despite scientists' claims to "solve" a problem, it is impossible to predict the impacts of even a single gene modification. Pleiotropic effects have included alterations in the crop's nutritional, toxic and allergenic properties. For example, a GM soya tested in 1996, had 27% higher levels of a major allergen, trypsin-inhibitor, than the non-GM parent variety. GM Bt insecticidal maize, tested in 2008, had an altered protein profile, including the appearance of a new form of the protein zein, which is a known allergen. See http://www.ncbi.nlm.nih.gov/pubmed/18393457

Even the new technique, called CRISPR, heralded for it's accuracy, still has unknown effects on non-targeted cells. CRISPR scientists rely on algorithms to predict the most obvious cell changes, but in a recent test case there were 100s of unforeseen effects—none of which would be picked up by the indadequate testing carried out to comply with GMO regulation.

For the scientists among us, this report (http://www.ncbi.nlm.nih.gov/pmc/articles/PMC1559911/) explores the mutational consequences of genetic engineering.

3. Contamination

GM crops can—and do—cross pollinate with wild and non-GM plants. Other sources of contamination are the inadvertent spread of seed by farm machinery, as well as mixing seeds during storage.

Cross pollination will not only contaminate wild plants, affecting their natural genetic makeup, but will seriously compromise any organic or non-GM farming system. Despite claims that GM and non-GM can co-exist, it is patently untrue.

Search the internet for "Co-existence of GM crops" and you will find a slew of papers which confirm the unrealistic claims of spatial regulation between pollinating crops. For economic and geographical constraints, farmers cannot be expected to isolate their GM crops. Organic farmers will lose their registration, and in Canada, for instance, it is now virtually impossible to cultivate non-GM oilseed rape, such is the overwhelming GM presence.

Recent examples from the Contamination Register include the arrival in the UK in 2015 of some genetically modified rape seed in a consignment of conventional seed from France. DEFRA was forced to destroy the crop and the consignment. Germany found GM Bt resistant rice in organic rice flour imported from China.

New genetic engineering techniques, such as CRISPr, increase the danger of plants with altered genes spreading throughout whole wild populations. A gene "drive" system allows for an edited gene on one chromosome to copy itself into its partner chromosome. The result is that nearly all offspring will inherit the engineered gene. If just a few organisms with gene drives are released into the wild, the whole population could end up with the edited gene.

> *"The regenerative Agriculture*
> *movement is growing with the goal of*
> *reversing climate change altogether."*

Regenerative Agriculture Can Undo the Harms of Traditional Agriculture

Kate Spring

Among the advantages cited for GMO crops—even by those who aren't totally comfortable with them—are their potential for continuing to produce even as the planet warms and extreme weather becomes more common. In the following viewpoint, Kate Spring proposes a different way agriculture can respond to climate change, and it is a very old and low-tech solution. Kate Spring is an organic farmer, mother, and chief inspiration officer at good heart farmstead in Worcester, Vermont. She contributes to the High Mowing Organic Seeds blog.

As you read, consider the following questions:

1. What does the author mean by the term "regenerative agriculture"?
2. How does regenerative agriculture actually improve soil?
3. In what way are the agricultural practices the author proposes one step better than merely avoiding GMOs?

"Regenerative Agriculture: Growing Techniques to Build Soil and Sequester Carbon," by Kate Spring, High Mowing Organic Seeds, January 30, 2017. Reprinted by permission.

In Vermont and across the country, climate change poses increasing challenges for farmers: flood and drought, unpredictable weather, increased pest pressure and new strains of diseases. At the same time, the agricultural sector is a leading cause of the greenhouse gasses that lead to climate change. It doesn't have to be, though. Just as the organic movement has offered an alternative to industrial agriculture, the Regenerative Agriculture movement is growing with the goal of reversing climate change altogether.

The organization regeneration international defines regenerative agriculture this way:

> The key to regenerative agriculture is that it not only "does no harm" to the land but actually improves it, using technologies that regenerate and revitalize the soil and the environment. Regenerative agriculture leads to healthy soil, capable of producing high quality, nutrient dense food while simultaneously improving, rather than degrading land, and ultimately leading to productive farms and healthy communities and economies.

I first came upon this movement thanks to livestock farming friends, who could draw a clear line between grazing animals and growing soil. As ungulates graze, they spread manure and aerate the soil, while poultry scratches at the upper layers of soil, helping integrate nutrients as they go. After grazing, the pasture regrows with the nutrients from the manure, and pulls carbon from the air, sending it underground through the roots.

Though different from grazing systems, vegetable farms, too, have a role to play in regenerative agriculture. Soil is the foundation of both organic and regenerative systems. To retain this fundamental building block, the regenerative vegetable farmer's main goals must be reducing soil loss and increasing organic matter.

Practical ways to reduce soil loss and keep the soil covered include:

Cover Cropping

Cover crops help reduce erosion and loss of nitrogen to the air while increasing organic matter. Some crops, like clover, field peas and vetch also add nitrogen while roots break up compacted soil. And like the grasses in a pasture, as cover crops grow they pull carbon into the soil through their roots. When incorporating cover crops into the soil, switch from tilling to mowing and harrowing the crops in order to decrease the disruption of soil structure and the release of soil carbon.

Sown Pathways

Pathways can leave soil exposed. Seed them in annual rye for a green pathway that requires minimal maintenance, smothers weeds, and increases organic matter. Straw or leaf mulch in pathways and on beds helps retain moisture and increase nutrients in the soil. As they break down, they will also add organic matter. Landscape fabric or plastic mulch helps retain moisture and cover the soil, and may be a more time efficient option for larger farms.

Plan Successions

Careful planning can decrease the time between crop successions. When transplanting, aim to pull one crop and plant another in the same day, both increasing your overall yield potential and decreasing the amount of time soil is left exposed.

A harder practice to implement on organic vegetable farms is no-till. Tilling has traditionally been one of the organic farmer's main ways to suppress weeds and incorporate plant residues. Though it achieves these means, it does so at a cost to the soil structure, leaving soil workable but without the structural integrity that increases its ability to retain water in times of drought and resist erosion in times of heavy rainfall or flood; most critically, tilling also releases carbon from the soil. No-till production methods help keep carbon sequestered and build organic matter at the same time.

For small farms, the transition to no-till can include these practices:

Permanent Bed System

Using a permanent bed system, the soil structure remains intact all season long. Consistent cultivation is important for weed management; on the upside, weed seeds are not brought up to the surface as they are during tilling. Over time, weed pressure may decrease using this management technique. Permanent bed systems work well with the use of plastic mulch or landscape fabric, which take away the need for cultivation.

Sheet Composting to Build Soil and Open New Space

This method of opening space requires the right timing and a willingness to prep fields without the use of a tractor, but can work well with permanent bed systems. In the fall, layer cardboard, compost, and leaves or straw. That's it—the cardboard will begin to breakdown through the winter, and the space will be ready for planting come spring or early summer. This prep can be done on specific beds to increase soil organic matter, or can be done over a larger area to create a new growing space for the following season.

Broadforking to Loosen and Aerate Soil

At Good Heart Farmstead, the broadfork is our most important tool, as every bed is broadforked before planting. The broadfork allows you to loosen the soil without inverting it, thereby keeping the soil structure intact. This subsequently increases the soil's ability to absorb and hold moisture, increasing resilience in both drought and flood.

Soil Solarization

Prep beds for new successions by cleaning out the old crop (either by flail-mowing or hand-pulling) and laying clear plastic over the bed(s). This heats up the soil, killing weed seeds and pathogens, and prepares the bed for a direct-seeded crop. At Good Heart, we use clear plastic when we want to turn a bed over quickly, mowing the previous crop and laying the plastic down on a sunny day, letting it heat the soil for 24–36 hours to increase the soil temperature to 85° in the first 2–3". We then pull up the plastic, rake off the residue and direct-seed. Alternatively, in the springtime when we want to prepare space in advance, we'll lay a silage tarp instead of clear plastic. This is most effective when left on for 4-6 weeks, giving time for weed seeds to germinate and die off, the soil temperature to increase, and to keep the soil covered until planting time arrives.

Use Compost to Prepare Beds for Direct Seeding

In place of tilling, rake a 1" layer of compost over the bed for a uniform, flat seeding area. This will increase your compost use, but it will also improve your soil (on our farm, we've found it helps with uniform germination as well). As with all inputs, it's wise to take a soil test each year to be sure your compost levels are appropriate.

At Good Heart Farmstead, we've swapped raking with running a power harrow on a BCS walk-behind tractor over the beds to increase efficiency. When transitioning a bed from one crop to another, our standard preparation is: flail mow, broadfork, spread compost, harrow, seed. Unlike a tiller, the power harrow works horizontally on the top inch of soil, creating an even, flat space without mixing soil layers. A tilther, which works only the top 2 inches of soil, is another option used on low-till farms.

While some refer to Regenerative Agriculture as "beyond organic", to me it harkens back to the foundation of organic farming: living soils and farming practices that enhance the health of land and people.

> *"It is in the developing world, however, especially in the areas of the world where yields are low due to the lack of technology, that biotechnology could have its greatest impact. It is very promising that several multinational companies are starting to takes steps to facilitate GM technology transfer."*

GMO Technology Should Be Transferred to the Developing World

Luis R. Herrera-Estrella

The following viewpoint dates all the way back to 2000. It is included here because it gives an insight into the development of GMOs. Although much of the data here is out of date (The UN now projects a world population of almost ten billion by 2050), this piece gives a sense of the excitement and urgency of the development of GMOs in the early days of the technology. In this viewpoint, the author focuses on the hopes that GMO crops will be the solution to a food crisis posed by the world's growing population. Luis Rafael Herrera-Estrella is a plant molecular biologist at Texas Tech University and a pioneer in the development of plant genetic engineering.

"Genetically Modified Crops and Developing Countries," by Luis R. Herrera-Estrella, The American Society of Plant Biologists, November 2000. Reprinted by permission.

As you read, consider the following questions:

1. Does knowing that the viewpoint was written more than 20 years ago make it seem naive to you? Why or why not?
2. After reading this viewpoint, does it seem to you that the arguments for GMO crops have changed? If so, how?
3. What problems with the implementation of this technology does the author foresee? Have these been addressed?

The world's population is expected to almost double by the year 2050, making food security the most important social issue for the next 30 years. Food production will have to be doubled or preferably tripled to meet the needs of the expected 6 billion people, 90% of whom will reside in the developing world. The enormity of this challenge will be further exacerbated by the dwindling availability of water and the fact that this additional food will have to be produced on existing agricultural land or marginal soils if forested regions and the environment as a whole are to be preserved.

There are numerous ways by which agricultural productivity may be increased in a sustainable way, including the use of biological fertilizers, improved pest control, soil and water conservation, and the use of improved plant varieties, produced by either traditional or biotechnological means. Of these measures, biotechnological applications, especially transgenic plant varieties and the future products of functional genomic projects, probably hold the most promise toward augmenting agricultural production and productivity when properly integrated into traditional systems.

The efficacy of transgenic plant varieties in increasing production and lowering production costs is already demonstrable. In 1996 and 1997, the cultivation of virus-, insect-, and herbicide-resistant plants accounted for a 5% to 10% increase in yield as well as for savings on herbicides of up to 40% and on insecticides of between $60 and $120 (US dollars) per acre (James, 1998).

However, these increases in productivity, impressive as they are, will probably have a limited impact on the global food supply because the products currently available on the market are suitable only for large mechanized farms practicing intensive agriculture. In fact, most of the transgenic crops that have been produced to date, especially by the private sector, are aimed either at reducing production costs in agricultural areas that already have high productivity levels or at increasing the value of the final product (e.g. improving the oil quality of seed crops).

In a global sense, a more effective strategy to ensure sufficient levels of food production would be to increase productivity in developing countries, especially in areas of subsistence farming, where an increase in food production is urgently needed and where crop yields are significantly lower than those obtained in other areas of the world. In developing countries in the tropics and subtropics, crop losses due to pests, diseases, and poor soils are made worse by climatic conditions that favor insect pests and disease vectors, and by the lack of economic resources to purchase high quality seeds, insecticides, and fertilizers. In addition to low productivity levels, post-harvest losses in tropical areas are very high due to the favorable climate for fungal and insect infestation and to the lack of appropriate storage facilities. Despite efforts to prevent pre- and post-harvest crop losses, pests destroy over half of all world crop production. Postharvest loss due to insects, the majority of which occurs in the developing world, is estimated to be 15% of the world's production. It is possible that many of these problems could be alleviated by plant biotechnology.

A major advantage of plant biotechnology is that it often generates strategies for crop improvement that can be applied to many different crops. Genetically engineered virus resistance, insect resistance, and delayed ripening are good examples of strategies that could potentially benefit a diversity of crops. Transgenic plants of over 20 plant species that are resistant to more than 30 different viral diseases have been produced using variations of the pathogen-derived resistance strategy. Insect-resistant plant varieties, using the δ-endotoxin of Bacillus thuringensis, have been produced for several important plant species, including tobacco, tomato, potato, cotton, walnut, maize, sugarcane, and rice. Of these, maize, potato, and cotton are already under commercial production. It is envisaged that these strategies can be used for many other crops important for tropical regions and other regions in the developing world. Genetically engineered delayed ripening, although only tested on a commercial scale for tomato, has an enormous potential application for tropical fruit crops, which suffer severe losses in developing countries because they ripen rapidly and because there is a lack of appropriate storage conditions and efficient transport systems for them to reach the final consumer.

A second advantage of plant biotechnology insofar as feeding the developing world is that in principle it does not require major changes in the agricultural practices of small farmers. To date, most of the developments in plant gene transfer technology and the different strategies to produce improved transgenic plant varieties have been driven by the economic value of the species or the trait. These economic values, in turn, are mainly determined by their importance to agriculture in the developed world, particularly the United States and western Europe. This is understandable: Substantial investments are needed to develop, field test, and commercialize new transgenic plant varieties. However, to increase global food production, it is necessary to ensure that this technology is effectively transferred to the developing world and adapted to local crops. Adapting biotechnology to local crops is an especially important consideration because indigenous crop species often have deep social and/or religious meaning to a culture, and simply replacing local crops with another crop to increase productivity could potentially destroy local cultural traditions. Moreover, traditional people are more likely to embrace a known crop with a genetic modification than a strange, foreign crop.

There are also problems that limit food production that are more or less specific to tropical and subtropical agriculture, but unfortunately these problems have not been deemed important enough to be studied intensively in developed countries. Because many of these problems are common to many countries and affect the productivity of a wide spectrum of crops, transgenic strategies that can be applied to different plant species to solve these problems are urgently needed. It is unfortunate that little is currently being done to address these problems. For instance, one of the major problems that affects plant productivity in tropical regions is soil acidity. Acidic soils comprise about 3.95 billion ha of the ice-free land or approximately 40% of the world's arable land, comprising about 68% of tropical America, 38% of tropical Asia, and 27% of tropical Africa (Pandey et al., 1994;Eswaran et al., 1997). In spite of its global importance, metal toxicity and nutrient deficiency problems that affect acid soils are investigated by only a handful of scientists in developed countries, and this topic has been largely neglected by large agrochemical companies.

It is a shame that in today's world, in which global food production should suffice to feed everyone, regardless of their religious, political, or geographical situation, many thousands of people starve to death and up to 800 million people are malnourished. How will we cope, then, with the increasing demand for food if technology is controlled by a few major companies, and the small farmers in developing countries, for want of economic resources, do not fall into the category of a potential consumer? In spite of what they might say, companies are not concerned with feeding the poor and arguably should not be. Companies are not charitable organizations: Their survival depends on the returns to their shareholders.

The fact that research and development in the private sector is driven by market considerations and not by philanthropic ideals is obvious in the case of tropical diseases. These diseases kill hundreds of thousands of people every year and, for many of them, vaccines have not yet been developed and current research is only done in public institutions. In many instances curing people is more profitable— and trendy—than preventing a disease. The power, but also the inhumane side, of research and development has perhaps been most clearly seen in the case of AIDS, for which new medicines that prevent the symptoms of this syndrome were developed in a few years of intense research after the first cases were reported in the United States. However, it is distressing to know that many thousands of people die every year from this terrible disease without having received the benefits of this research, simply because they have no money. Because people in rich countries are no longer seeing their friends die of AIDS and transmission of the disease is pretty much under control, the activism seen in the United States and Europe to force governments to increase the research and development budget to find AIDS cures or vaccines has to a large extent disappeared when, in reality, more people die of AIDS than ever before and the number of infected people increases daily.

In the case of food, a similar but more dramatic scenario can be foreseen. Hundreds or even thousands of millions of people in the coming decades will have an urgent need for food, but the technology needed to produce their supplies locally might not reach them. Not only will food availability be a major problem in the next few decades, but the world's environment will become increasingly at risk. In spite of the fact that tropical forests are invaluable to local, regional, and global ecosystems and critical to maintaining biodiversity (over 90% of plant and animal species live in forest ecosystems), approximately 11 million ha of forest are cleared every year by farmers searching for more productive land. Indiscriminate conversion of tropical forest into agricultural land will have more far-reaching ecological consequences than the use of genetically modified (GM) crops.

To ensure the transfer of technology that will maximize food production and preserve the environment, several economic, political, and social issues must be dealt with. It is my personal opinion that an ultimate failure to end hunger in developing countries will arise not from technological limitations but from political and/or economic decisions and the disinterest of governments and corporations. In this regard, perhaps an international body could be created to facilitate the transfer of the necessary technology to places where it would prove most useful. United Nations Education has already established a precedent for such a body when it agreed that certain designated regions and cities of the world should be preserved not just for the benefit of the local people but for all of humanity. Perhaps a similar concept could be applied in terms of new technology. Technology that addresses fundamental problems of human well-being should be given a special status to ensure that it reaches everyone.

The transfer of this technology to developing nations will, of course, engender problems. For instance, under what circumstances can royalties be waived? One approach, perhaps naive, would be to reach agreements in which the technology is donated on a royalty-free basis if it will only be used for production aimed at the internal markets of developing countries. In these cases, when export is possible, royalties should, of course, be paid; if the farmers can export their products, they should share the extra profits with the providers of the technology.

It is very unfortunate that the decision of whether this technology is going to be further developed and transferred to the small farmer is not in the hands of people in the developing world but in those of large multinational companies and the consumers and governments of developed countries. Consumer groups in Europe claim their right to choose whether they want GM food or not. They also raise the question: Why do we bother at all with GM food if we have more than enough food already? The remaining questions are: Will the poor have the choice to use genetic engineering? Will they have the opportunity to decide whether they want to eat or not? Will political and economic interests, with or without GM food, allow us to reach the levels of food production necessary to feed the growing world population?

It is unfortunate that most developing countries do not have sufficient resources to implement the necessary biotechnological solutions to the major problems that limit agricultural productivity, at least not in the required time frame. It is in the developing world, however, especially in the areas of the world where yields are low due to the lack of technology, that biotechnology could have its greatest impact. It is very promising that several multinational companies are starting to takes steps to facilitate GM technology transfer.

References

1. Moniz ACEswaran H, Reich P, Beinroth F (1997) Global distribution of soils with acidity. in *Plant-Soil Interactions at Low pH*. Brazilian Soil Science Society, Sao Paulo, Brazil, ed Moniz AC pp 159–164.

2. James C (1998) Update in the development and commercialisation of genetically modified crops. *Int Serv Acquisition Agrobiotechnol Appl Briefs* 5:1–20.

3. Edmeades GE, Deutsch JAPandey S, Ceballos H, Granados G, Knapp E (1994) Developing maize that tolerates aluminum toxic soils. in *Stress Tolerance Breeding: Maize That Resist Insects, Drought, Low Nitrogen and Acidic Soils. International Center for Development of Maize and Wheat, Texcoco, Mexico*, eds Edmeades GE, Deutsch JA pp 60–73.

Periodical and Internet Sources Bibliography

The following articles have been selected to supplement the diverse views presented in this chapter.

Artem Anyshchenko, "How should we regulate GMOs? Regulation of GMOs must accommodate both scientific developments and public perception of the risks associated with biotechnology," *Science Nordic*, 23 March 2017. https://sciencenordic.com/ agriculture-biotech-denmark/how-should-we-regulate-gmos/1443831

Omri Ben-Shahar, "The Environmentalist Case in Favor of GMO Food," *Forbes*, 26 February 2018. https://www.forbes.com/sites/ omribenshahar/2018/02/26/the-environmentalist-case-in-favor-of-gmo-food/#2e679f2937de

James Hamblin, "The Fading Meaning of GMO: The National Academy of Sciences Is Urging People to Focus Less on the Process and More on the Product," *Atlantic*, 17 May 2016. https:// www.theatlantic.com/science/archive/2016/05/plants-for-the-planet/483132/

Ferris Jabr, "Organic GMOs Could Be the Future of Food—If We Let Them," *Wired*, 7 October 2015. https://www.wired.com/2015/10/ organic-gmos-could-be-the-future-of-food-if-we-let-them/

Michael Le Page, "Colonists Could Use Genetically Modified Bacteria to Settle Mars," 21 June 2018, https://www.newscientist.com/ article/2172270-colonists-could-use-genetically-modified-bacteria-to-settle-mars/

Caroline Newman, "Largest-Ever Study Reveals Environmental Impact of Genetically Modified Crops," *UVA Today*, 14 September 2016. https://news.virginia.edu/content/largest-ever-study-reveals-environmental-impact-genetically-modified-crops

Brad Plumer, "Are GMO Crops Good or Bad for the Environment?' Vox, 22 July 2015 https://www.vox.com/2014/11/3/18092738/are-gm-crops-good-or-bad-for-the-environment

Michael Specter, "Could Genetically Modified Mosquitoes Save Hawaii's Endangered Birds?" *New Yorker*, 9 September 2016. https://www.newyorker.com/news/daily-comment/could-genetically-modified-mosquitoes-save-hawaiis-endangered-birds

OPPOSING
VIEWPOINTS®
SERIES

Are Genetically Modified Foods Necessary to Feed the World's Growing Population?

Chapter Preface

In this chapter's viewpoints, the authors turn to a more subtle question. Not, "are GMOs safe," so much as "are they necessary?" Despite a world in which people in some nations are dying from obesity, much of the world still lacks enough food, or they lack food that is nutritious enough to ensure good health.

With the world population continuing to increase, it will take creative solutions to be sure there is enough food to feed everyone. In this chapter, viewpoint authors tackle the question of how best to do that. Are genetically engineered foods the answer? Are genetically engineered foods the only hope or are there better, safer solutions? Are GMOs *really* necessary to feed the world? (Note that because the world population is growing rapidly, the population statistics and estimates given in the viewpoints vary depending on when the piece was written.)

The issue is not as straightforward as it sounds. As with any technology, there are risks and benefits to be weighed. And especially with bioengineering, there is still much we don't know about the long-term consequences of genetically modified foods. The authors in this chapter acknowledge these concerns and agree that the problem of world hunger demands solutions.

They disagree only on what those solutions should be. On the one hand, some people are convinced that we have the technology to provide more nutritious, more productive crops. To prevent these crops from being grown and brought to market, they say, is to essentially deny hungry people a source of food. Others argue that the problem of world hunger is much more complex than simply producing enough food. Political and logistical problems in getting food to those who need it have as much to do with hunger as does lack of food production. The risks and benefits must also be weighed, they say. And, as with any discussion about agriculture, the issue of climate change is considered, as well.

> *"Using genetic engineering to biofortify crops is not a panacea, but it does offer an important alternative."*

Genetically Engineered Foods Can Save Lives

Daniel Norero

In the following viewpoint, Daniel Norero begins by pointing out the need for solutions to worldwide nutritional deficiency. He explains why previous programs to address this problem have not been successful enough. Here, he proposes the use of genetically biofortified plants to enhance the nutritional content of crops in areas with nutritional deficiency. Daniel Norero is a consultant in scientific communication at agricultural biotechnology and food-tech institutions and a columnist in the Chilean media "El Definido." He founded the initiative "Yo Quiero transgénicos" (I Do Want GMOs), a citizen project that aims to demystify and inform about GMOs, with special emphasis on biotech crops in Latin America.

"Unfairly Demonized GMO Crops Can Help Fight Malnutrition," by Daniel Norero, Cornell Alliance for Science, June 20, 2018. Reprinted by permission.

As you read, consider the following questions:

1. What is the problem that the author hopes genetically engineered crops can potentially solve?
2. What are Golden Rice and the "super" banana, and how are these foods made?
3. What, according to this viewpoint, is holding up the use of potentially life-saving foods such as Golden Rice?

About 800 million people are currently suffering from hunger in the world, and some 2 billion suffer from some type of important nutritional deficiency. Addressing global food security becomes essential when the population is projected to increase to 9.6 billion by 2050. This will require a global food supply increase of 70 percent, as well as more nutritious foods, especially for countries with problems of nutritional deficiency.

Strategies to combat this have included international food aid programs that provide supplements through pills, or fortification of local foods in the processing phase. However, the success of these efforts has been limited, due to such factors as inconsistent external funding and limited purchasing power and access to markets and hospitals by poor populations.

Another promising strategy—one that dodges these challenges and offers long-term sustainability—has been using plant breeding programs to develop staple crops with higher nutrient levels. These biofortified crops allow people to access specific nutrients through their daily diet, such as rice in Asia, sorghum and banana in Africa, or corn in Latin America. In this way, biofortified crops are an important alternative to alleviate malnutrition in the world.

The biofortification of crops can be achieved through conventional breeding or genetic engineering. Despite its success, conventional breeding is limited to closely related (sexually compatible) plants, and therefore directly depends on the natural variation of the nutrient of interest. It also requires a lot of time to stabilize the desired trait. Although certain techniques of modern biotechnology can accelerate conventional breeding, the minimum number of generations needed for clonal propagation crops—for example, potatoes, sweet potato, banana and cassava—is estimated at seven generations. For self-fertilizing crops, such as rice, wheat and sorghum, nine generations are required, and for cross-pollinated crops, such as corn, it increases to 17 generations.

Also, breeding strategies with genetic engineering can be redirected towards the accumulation of a non-existent target nutrient in a desired tissue, such as the cereal endosperm, without compromising the micronutrient content in the milling process.

So far, much progress has been made in increasing the vitamin content in staple crops through this approach. An example is biofortification with beta-carotene, the precursor of vitamin A, which is highly important for the normal functioning of vision and the immune system. Globally, the severe deficiency of this vitamin causes 500,000 cases of irreversible blindness, millions of cases of xerophthalmia, and up to 2 million deaths per year, most of these in children under 5 years of age.

The first genetically modified (GM) crop that produced beta-carotene was rice, an important cereal that doesn't have this nutrient in its grain. Known as "Golden Rice," its current version was initially obtained after an insertion of a gene from a bacterium and another from maize. About 150 grams of this rice provides the recommended amount of vitamin A for a child.

This technology was developed for humanitarian purposes by a public-private consortium that released the patent for use in developing countries. It also has passed different biosafety and human consumption tests, and been approved for human consumption by the regulatory agencies of four developed countries. Unfortunately, it has not yet been authorized for cultivation in any of the countries where it is needed. This is partly due to the excessive regulation of GM crops and the strong opposition of environmental movements.

Another example is the "golden banana," developed by an Australian researcher who inserted a banana gene from Papua New

Guinea, and another from bacteria, in the Cavendish banana—the most popular variety worldwide. The technology developed in Australia is transferred to a group of public researchers in Uganda, who are modifying the EAHB and Sukali Ndizi varieties, the two most consumed in Africa. Currently, both beta-carotene and iron levels continue to increase, and a human consumption test is underway in the United States. This "super banana" was named one of Time Magazine's 25 Best Inventions of 2014, and like golden rice, the technology will be released without royalties so that it can be cultivated freely by African farmers.

Genetic engineering has also significantly increased beta-carotene in crops such as potatoes, cassava, wheat, oranges, soybean, cauliflower, melon, apples and others—all of them developed by public entities and universities.

Other important nutrients are folic acid, or folate, and iron. For the case of folate, Belgian researchers achieved an increase of 150-fold in rice. This rice could significantly reduce the risk of birth defects, such as spina bifida and other conditions of neural tube defects, caused by a deficiency of this nutrient. A Brazilian state company, EMBRAPA, also managed to increase folate 15-fold in lettuce—two leaves of that GM lettuce could provide 100 percent of the daily requirement for an adult. Additionally, EMBRAPA—in collaboration with a Mexican university—developed a GM bean with 84-fold more folic acid. In the case of iron, important increases have been achieved in rice, wheat and maize.

There are also GM crops where several nutrients have been increased, such as an African corn that was modified by researchers from a Spanish university, achieving 169 times more beta-carotene, six times more vitamin C and twice as much folate. During 2014, animal consumption tests were carried out, and in 2015 human consumption tests were being carried out as well as an experimental field trial. A second example is GM sorghum produced by the "Biofortified Sorghum Project for Africa". This public-private partnership has managed to increase the level of beta-carotene, iron, zinc and essential amino acids, and field and greenhouse trials have already been carried out in the United States and Africa [25]. These crops have the objective of alleviating nutritional deficiency in underdeveloped countries of Africa.

Using genetic engineering to biofortify crops is not a panacea, but it does offer an important alternative. It should not be rejected as it has proven to be a useful tool to complement and/or improve conventional breeding programs.

On the other hand, the lack of regulatory frameworks for biosafety laws that allow the use of GM crops in several developing countries, or the excessive regulation in which they already have a defined framework, should be re-evaluated. Golden Rice is an example of how a technology for humanitarian purposes can be delayed for more than a decade, in part due to excessive regulation. In India alone, the cost of not commercializing Golden Rice was more than US$199 million annually and the loss of 1.4 million lives in the last decade. Let's not increase these dismal statistics. Instead, regulators and political leaders in developing nations need to move forward in approving these nutritious and safe crops to improve health and save lives.

> *"Industry studies show that it takes a minimum of ten years to develop a GE crop and nearly $150 million; whereas conventional crops take only $1 million to develop."*

GMOs Are Not Necessary to Feed the World

Green America

The previous viewpoint argued for the benefits of genetically modified crops. In the following viewpoint Green America argues that traditional plant breeding can achieve the same benefits without the risks of GMOs. In addition, the author argues for an approach called agroecology, which will help solve not only hunger but environmental problems as well. Green America is a membership-based non-profit organization that works to use the strength of consumers, investors, businesses, and the marketplace to create a socially just and environmentally sustainable society.

As you read, consider the following questions:

1. What are the problems with using GM crops to decrease losses due to pests in an attempt to increase crop yields, according to the viewpoint?
2. How does this viewpoint define "agroecology"?
3. What are some of the factors listed as contributing to world hunger?

O ne of the most often touted benefits of genetically engineered (GE) crops [more commonly referred to as genetically modified organisms (GMOs)] is that they are essential to feed the world's growing population. There are currently over 7.5 billion people on this planet and expected to rise to 9.5 billion by 2050. If consumption trends continue, in order to feed that many people, we would need to grow one-third more food. First, let's look at this argument from an agricultural perspective.

The vast majority of GE crop production does not go towards direct food consumption; rather, it is used for the production of animal feed and ethanol. These are crops engineered to withstand, work in partnership with, and self-generate pesticides. They are not engineered to increase yield or face climate-related challenges to growth, such as drought tolerance. There is one variety of corn has been bred for drought resistance, but it is likely to only be effective in 15 percent of US corn fields and is not effective in severe or extreme drought, which we are expected to have more of in the coming years.

Industrial Agriculture Isn't the Answer

Increases in yield from GE crops are a result of a decrease in yield lost to pests from Bt crops, pesticides, and an increase in fertilizer use (made from petroleum, defeating the purpose of ethanol). Unfortunately, growing weed and pest resistance is already decreasing their effectiveness, requiring much more dangerous pesticides and making useless one of the most used organic pesticides, Bt. These minimal increases in yield have come with major externalities, including but not limited to water pollution, pollinator loss, and soil degradation, that put future food security at risk. After decades of attempts, Big Biotech has not been successful in breeding GE seeds that increase yield or reduce water use. Conventional breeding outperforms genetic engineering when it comes to nitrogen use efficiency (the ability for crops to pull nitrogen out of soil, developing a more efficient use of fertilizer, ultimately decreasing the demand for fertilizers) and water use efficiency (WUE).

Overall, conventional breeding is responsible for most of the successful advances in yield. It also happens on a much shorter timeline at a much lower cost. Industry studies show that it takes a minimum of ten years to develop a GE crop and nearly $150 million; whereas conventional crops take only $1 million to develop, improvements WUE and drought resistance naturally occur at an estimated 1 percent each year. While Big Biotech develop GE crops in a lab, farmers are improving traditional crops in the field. Due to this drag rate by the time GE crops are finally released they are actually behind their conventional counterparts.

Conventional crops could also be more effectively bred to work in partnership with the cultural food needs and geographical climate and soil challenges unique to specific regions. Forcing GE crops into developing countries with higher existing biodiversity puts that biodiversity and future food supplies at risk by threatening native species and practices. There are an abundance of types of crop varieties (both already in use and wild) accessible to breeders and growers. It is important that we tap into this vast resource to expand nutrient diversity and accessibility.

The Solution: Agroecology

Considering the changing climate and increasing pressures on and demand for our scarce resources, expanding the industrialized system of agricultural is not the answer. Agriculture is already one of the largest contributors to climate change. In order to sustainability produce the food we will need, we must support a transition to more regenerative, agroecological methods of farming. Agroecology as a "science is the 'application of ecological science to the study, design, and management of sustainable agroecosystems.' As a set of agricultural practices, agroecology seeks ways to enhance agricultural systems by mimicking natural processes, thus creating beneficial biological interactions and synergies among the components of the agroecosystem."

It is essential to look at the entire system and how plants work with one another and their surrounding climates. Regenerative agriculture works to rebuild soil health and biodiversity; sequestering carbon, preventing soil erosion, protecting water sources, and reducing harmful pesticide and fertilizer runoff in the process. Agroecology is also a much better system of management for small holders and provides a more balanced diet with more nutrient dense crops. Smallholders already produce 70 percent of the world's food on only 25 percent of the land. More diversified planting is better for soil health and biodiversity and will better handle the challenges presented by climate change and the damage we have already done to our resources.

Lack of Equity + Poverty = Hunger

Hunger is not an issue of agriculture or food quantity, but one of poverty and equity. There is currently enough food in the world to feed 10 billion people. That means that we actually have an excess of food.

Despite that, there is still a shocking number of people who are hungry, 791 million (the majority of which live in developing nations). More than anything, hunger is a result of poverty. The World Bank estimates that there are over 1 billion poor people in developing countries. Continued hunger leads to continued poverty as those suffering from chronic hunger are unable to perform manual labor (the most common source of income in developing countries) and increase their standard of living. Much of this poverty and hunger is caused by existing economic inequity as a result of current political systems that favor those with higher incomes. The current industrial food system emphasizes the need for countries (regardless of size) to export food crops despite the local demand for basic nutrients. If poverty and livelihoods are not improved it will not matter how much food is produced if the poorest, and in turn hungriest, do not have the financial ability to access it.

At the same time that there is great hunger there is also excessive food waste throughout the world. It is even worse in the western hemisphere; the US alone wastes 40 percent of its food. In western countries, grocery stores throw out a lot of food and will not purchase unattractive produce. Food is wasted simply because it is visually unappealing or goes uneaten. In developing nations food waste is a result of a lack of infrastructure, capital investment, and basic necessities. Lack of access to road ways, storage facilities, and basic refrigeration prevents food access and increases spoilage rates. With proper investment and support these problems could be remedied.

Despite the hunger epidemic we also have an obesity epidemic as a result of poor nutrition, high meat consumption, and increased processed food consumption. Worldwide, most of the expected demand for an increase in food is not based on a baseline need for nutrients, but rather the growing trend of developing countries to adopt the western diet of meat consumption. It takes substantially more calories to produce meat and ultimately results in a number of health challenges. Not only does this require a higher production of animal feed crops, the raising of animals for meat puts a number of stresses on the environment due to the current system of large concentrated and confined animal feeding operations, or CAFOs.

Hunger Is an Issue of Politics and Justice

It is a choice that we make as a nation and as group of developed countries. In order to tackle these problems of access we need to drastically change our food system. We need an international system of agriculture that supports food sovereignty, regenerative agroecological farming practices, and food security on a regional and local level. GMOs are not the answer.

> *"Climate change may mean that the crops we depend on now may no longer be suited to the areas where they are currently cultivated and may increasingly be threatened by droughts, floods and the spread of plant diseases due to altered weather patterns."*

GMO Crops May Help Solve Problems Created by Climate Change

Stuart Thompson

In the following viewpoint, Stuart Thompson argues that genetically modified crops may be necessary to feed the world. Crops can be engineered to withstand the challenges of climate change. By transferring drought and disease resistance traits from some plants to other that lack these traits, via gene editing, crops can be tweaked to thrive in whatever conditions present themselves in a rapidly changing climate. Stuart Thompson is senior lecturer in plant biochemistry at the University of Westminster in London.

As you read, consider the following questions:

1. According to the author, what traits do many plants already have that would allow food crops to adapt to climate change?
2. What are some of the challenges the author describes in transferring beneficial traits from one plant species to another?
3. What "less ambitious" approaches does the author suggest?

T he United Nations forecasts global population to rise to more than 9 billion people by 2050. Climate change may mean that the crops we depend on now may no longer be suited to the areas where they are currently cultivated and may increasingly be threatened by droughts, floods and the spread of plant diseases due to altered weather patterns. So feeding everyone in the coming decades will be a challenge—can genetically modified crops help us achieve this?

Two groups of genetically modified crops are widely grown. The first are altered so that they are not affected by the herbicide glyphosate, which means that farmers can eliminate weeds without harming their crop. Glyphosate-resistant crops can increase farming efficiency but, while helping to get rid of weeds, herbicide resistance has no direct effect on the quantity of food produced, so their contribution to food security is likely to be limited.

The second type produce a natural insecticide inside the parts of the plant that pests eat. This protects the yields of these crops against insect infestation, which is arguably more environmentally friendly than using sprays that could be toxic to other organisms. Crops of this type are likely to be useful, but we should increase the number of insecticide genes that we employ to prevent evolution of resistant pests.

Farmers have always faced crop diseases—think of the Irish potato famine of the 19th century—and some scientists predict that climate change may allow previously contained infections to spread into new areas and become more damaging. It may already have contributed to the devastating appearance of a fungal infection called wheat blast in Bangladesh, a disease that can cause nearly complete loss of this critical crop in infected fields.

Disease Resistance

Genetic modification can certainly be used in the fight to make crops more disease resistant. Many plants are vulnerable to an infection because they cannot detect the invading organism. However, the proteins that identify an infection and activate a plant's defences can be moved between varieties or even species using genetic modification. This will enable previously vulnerable crops to turn on resistance mechanisms.

It is also becoming possible to rewrite the genes for these gatekeeper proteins so that they work for different diseases. A powerful and rapid method for editing genes called CRISPR-Cas9 has recently been developed and it is already being harnessed to produce genetically modified crops. For example, genes that make wheat vulnerable to powdery mildew have been changed to produce a resistant variety.

Nor is gene editing limited to improving disease resistance. Tomatoes have been tweaked to be insensitive to changes in the number of hours of sunlight in a day. This causes them to produce fruit more quickly because they aren't waiting for the right time of year to start flowering.

Improving Photosynthesis

Fundamentally, agriculture uses photosynthesis to convert light energy, water and carbon dioxide into food—so improving this process would increase how much food we produce. An obvious target is the step that captures carbon dioxide as it sometimes mistakes oxygen for carbon dioxide in a wasteful set of reactions called photorespiration.

GMOs Increase Global Food Security by Reducing Food Waste

People may be condemning potentially lifesaving technology before they have all the information. GMOs can be the catalyst for increased global food security.

Right now 60 percent of fruits and vegetables don't get eaten. This is due in part to poor collection techniques, small windows to harvest, transportation, and them simply going bad before people can eat them.

Potato bruising alone costs the industry at least $289 million annually. Earlier in 2015, after over a decade in development, Simplot's Innate Potato received FDA approval. This potato doesn't bruise or blacken as easily, is resistant to the Late Blight pathogens, and can be stored for longer. This is huge. Some of the biggest losses in the industry come from bruising during transportation. If that can be reduced, even marginally, the results will help people. And that's what this is all really about isn't it?

Advances in alternative forms of pest control and temperature mitigation are also getting better every day. The implementation of forms of Trichoderma, a genus of fungi found in soil, can make a huge difference in the life expectancy of crops. They form a symbiotic relationship with crops that can delay or prevent diseases, or increase the growth and yield of crops such as wheat.

People have demonized GMOs, slandered and condemned them, without knowing the whole truth. Crops that last longer, can be harvested later, and those that resist disease are a way to step up and feed the countless hungry people in this world. It's time to stop worrying, and love the GMO.

"GMOs Reduce Food Waste, Increase Global Food Security," by Gus Stahl, The Genetic Literacy Project, September 21, 2015.

As it happens, some plants already have a solution to this problem. They possess a system that pumps carbon dioxide into specialised parts of the leaf where most photosynthesis occurs, concentrating it there so that photorespiration doesn't happen. These species, known as C4 plants, can make more use of sunlight at higher temperatures and need less water because the pores that let carbon dioxide into their leaves don't have to open so much and therefore less water vapour escapes through them.

It has been estimated that transferring these mechanisms into other crop species such as rice could increase productivity by 50%. Unfortunately, progress towards this goal has been slow, partly because rice doesn't have the same leaf structure as C4 plants. A version of rice that can carry out a simple version of C4 photosynthesis has recently been produced but it will take at least ten years to optimise it.

Less ambitious approaches may provide benefits more quickly, such as a new type of wheat in which productivity has been increased by 15% to 20% by speeding up recycling of ribulose bisphosphate which is crucial for carbon dioxide capture.

Improving Nutrition

Crops are not just being genetically modified to improve their quantity but also their nutritional quality. The most prominent of these is "golden rice". Vitamin A deficiency causes 250,000 deaths per year and is common in populations whose diet is heavily dependent on rice. Golden rice is golden because it produces large quantities of yellow dietary carotenoids that our bodies can convert into vitamin A.

Other "biofortified" crops in development include potatoes with more protein and cooking bananas with increased carotenoids and iron.

Many people—and countries—are still sceptical about GM food. But people and animals have now been consuming GM crops for more than 20 years without apparent harm to their health. On the other hand, there is no question that starvation kills and that food insecurity is a major global threat. There are challenging times ahead. Can we afford to close the door on these powerful ways to protect our food supply?

> *"Farmers in Africa already have effective approaches to seed and agriculture, which are far more environmentally and farmer-friendly than GM."*

GM Crops Won't Help African Farmers

Million Belay

In the following viewpoint, Million Belay offers an African perspective on GM foods. The author argues that, contrary to what many others have claimed, GM crops are not the solution to hunger in developing countries. He responds specifically to a speech that had been recently made by Owen Patterson, who was at that time the UK's Environment Minister. But as you've seen, it is a claim frequently made by those who are grappling with this issue of GMOs. Million Belay is coordinator of the Alliance for Food Sovereignty in Africa.

As you read, consider the following questions:

1. According to the author, what approaches do African farmers already have for growing enough food to feed their nations?
2. How has the so-called Green Revolution actually hurt African farmers, according to the viewpoint?
3. What would be the consequences of GM crops in Africa?

"GM Crops Won't Help African Farmers," by Million Belay, Guardian News and Media Limited, June 24, 2013. Reprinted by permission.

Last week we heard that Owen Paterson, the UK's environment minister, is claiming that GM crops are necessary to help address hunger in developing countries, and that it would be immoral for Britain not to help developing countries to take up GM. Millions of small-scale farmers in Africa would disagree. African farmers and civil society have repeatedly rejected GM crops, and asked their governments to ban them.

Paterson does not appear to understand the complex realities and challenges of farming in Africa. Nor does he seem to grasp the limitations of GM crops. He fails to recognise that farmers in Africa already have effective approaches to seed and agriculture, which are far more environmentally and farmer-friendly than GM. Most of all, he fails to acknowledge the devastating impact that GM crops will have on African farmers and farming systems.

In the UK, Africa is often talked about as a failing continent where the hungry apparently wait around for northern benefactors to save us. Talk of Africa seems to imply that we have little or no food production, that our farmers are clueless, our seed unproductive. We won't go into how patronising and insulting this attitude is. Instead, we will focus on how this failure to acknowledge African farming systems and seed is being used to wipe them out.

Traditional African farming systems have developed an incredible diversity of seed varieties, which are able to deal with the multiple challenges of farming. Seed breeding is a complex art, and scientists who really listen and engage will realise that African farmers have a vast amount of ecological knowledge. Having many different types of seed—bred for their flavours and better nutrition, and which have evolved with local pests and diseases and are adapted to different soils and weather patterns—is a far better strategy of resilience than developing a single crop that is bound to fail in the face of climate change.

It is a myth that the green revolution has helped poor farmers. By pushing just a few varieties of seed that need fertilisers and pesticides, agribusiness has eroded our indigenous crop diversity. It is not a solution to hunger and malnutrition, but a cause. If northern governments genuinely wish to help African agriculture, they should support the revival of seed-saving practices, to ensure that there is diversity in farmers' hands.

But GM crops pose an even greater threat to Africa's greatest wealth. GM companies make it illegal to save seed. We have seen that farmers in North America whose crop was cross-pollinated by GM pollen have been sued by the GM company. About 80% of African small-scale farmers save their seed. How are they supposed to protect the varieties they have developed, crossed and shared over generations from GM contamination? This will be a disaster for them.

Paterson refers to the use of GM cotton in India. But he fails to mention that GM cotton has been widely blamed for an epidemic of suicides among Indian farmers, plunged into debt from high seed and pesticide costs, and failing crops.

Paterson also refers to the supposed potential of GM crops developed to be drought-tolerant. These crops are not yet on the market, and we don't know if they ever will be. The only two varieties of GM that have been sold in the past 15 years are resistant to a particular type of pest and a particular type of herbicide. Ask farmers if stalk borers or weeds are a cause of hunger in Africa, and they will laugh at you.

Instead of waiting for expensive GM solutions that may never arrive—and will ruin us if they do—we have worked with communities who were able to produce surplus food in times of drought by returning to their traditional varieties. A long-term study in Ethiopia showed that crops fare much better in an environment where soil and water is conserved in composted land than on land that is pumped full of fertiliser and imported seeds. Communities increasingly understand that modern seeds often fail in these times of changing climates and unpredictable weather. The only way to ensure real food security is to support farmers to revive their seed diversity and healthy soil ecology.

As Esther Bett, a farmer from Eldoret in Kenya, said last week: "It seems that farmers in America can only make a living from

GM crops if they have big farms, covering hundreds of hectares, and lots of machinery. But we can feed hundreds of families off the same area of land using our own seed and techniques, and many different crops. Our model is clearly more efficient and productive. Mr Paterson is wrong to pretend that these GM crops will help us at all."

> *"Critics of crop biotechnology misrepresent the evidence that shows that GMOs can help developing countries combat hunger in numerous, specific ways."*

The Complex Problem of Food Scarcity Will Need an Equally Complex Solution

Genetic Literacy Project

In the following viewpoint, the Genetic Literacy Project specifically addresses the implication made in the previous viewpoint that agricultural biotech companies are trying to boost profits at the expense of developing nations. The issue is complex, they say, and so are the solutions, which might include both GM crops and small-scale farming techniques, such as the ones mentioned in the previous viewpoint. GMO advocates, they say, never claimed that GMOs alone could feed the world. However, they do argue that GMOs are an essential part of the solution. The Genetic Literacy Project is a nonprofit organization dedicated to promoting genetics, biotechnology, evolution, and science literacy. It was formerly funded by Monsato, the controversial biotech corporation.

"Are GMOs Necessary to Feed the World?" Science Literacy Project. Reprinted by permission.

As you read, consider the following questions:

1. What is a "straw man argument"?
2. How do these authors say critics of biotechnology are misrepresenting the evidence for GMOs?
3. Why, according to this viewpoint are economic growth and agroecology no longer adequate solutions?

"The human population has grown at a breakneck pace and threatens to further exacerbate a problem that has worsened in recent years: chronic hunger. Genetically modified crops could help to relieve this problem by providing increased yields and being more resistant to environmental stressors."

—Christopher Gerry, Department of Chemistry and Chemical Biology, Harvard University

"The companies that develop and market GMOs may promise that they will produce greater yields and solve the world's food shortages, but …. GMO yields are hardly keeping pace with non-GMO crops."

—Just Label It, organic industry advocacy group

One of the most contentious aspects of the GMO debate is whether biotechnology is necessary to meet the food consumption needs of the world's growing population, expected to near 10 billion by 2050. During the same period, food demands by the existing population in the developing world are expected to soar by 50% or more. To meet this food security challenge, experts estimate that agricultural production needs to roughly double in the coming decades. How can that be achieved?

Agricultural scientists and many independent humanitarian organizations such as the Gates Foundation and the United Nations argue that GMOs (and soon gene editing) are critical tools to help farmers increase yields, combat pests and adapt to shifting climates. Critics mock this view, saying, "GMOs are not necessary to feed the world"—a definitive claim biotech advocates never actually make. Critics challenge the scientific consensus that genetically engineered crops increase yields. GMOs threaten the sovereignty of developing countries, they say, maintaining that the food shortage crisis is a myth promoted by "big ag" to boost their profits under the guise of doing noble humanitarian work. Rather, organic and agroecological farming and infrastructure investment to improve food distribution could adequately alleviate world hunger and growing food demands.

Most agriculture experts say this argument oversimplifies the food security challenge. World hunger is a complex problem. Multiple tools, including small-scale farming in certain situations, intensive farming in others and the sustainability advantages and increased yields of many genetically engineered crops should be accessible to farmers.

Science and Politics

Beginning in 1944, geneticist and plant pathologist Norman Borlaug led an initiative called the Cooperative Wheat Research and Production Program, which developed disease-resistant wheat varieties in Mexico. The research launched a period of dramatic growth in agricultural production that became known as the "Green Revolution." Borlaug's work increased food production so much in fact that a billion people in Latin America, the Middle East and Africa avoided starvation.

Trying to build on the Green Revolution, proponents of crop biotechnology have noted that GMOs, which have been shown to increase yields over organic conventional farming by 15-40%, could help bring a Green Revolution to Africa and other parts of the developing world.

Anti-GMO activists have caricatured this argument as part of their broader strategy of demonizing crop biotechnology. "One of the most often touted benefits of GMOs is that they are essential to feed the world's growing population," the organic-supporting advocacy group Green America posts on its website. "Claims that GMOs will 'feed the world' don't hold up," Environmental Working Group, a nonprofit funded by the organic food industry, posts.

It's a strawman argument, however. No scientist claims that GMOs by themselves can "feed the world." GMOs have been shown to increase crop yields over both conventional and organic agriculture and use less synthetic chemical inputs than non-GMO conventional farming. GMOs are one tool among many. More importantly, estimates indicate that we are farming approximately half of the available land on earth suitable for growing food, and almost all of the prime arable land. Very little of the prime land exists in the developing world, meaning biotechnology will be key in producing crops that can grow in less fertile soil.

Mischaracterizing the supplemental but key role biotechnology plays in producing more food at lower costs allows anti-GMO advocates to promote the alleged benefits of organic farming. Green America:

> In order to sustainability produce the food we will need, we must support .... agroecological methods of farming .... agroecology seeks ways to enhance agricultural systems by mimicking natural processes, thus creating beneficial biological interactions and synergies among the components of the agroecosystem.

But this promotion of agroecology ignores the large body of evidence that confirms biotechnology's role in producing more food. An April 2018 analysis of 6,000 studies, covering 21 years of data, concluded that genetic engineering increased corn yields by 25 percent, and provided more nutritious food as an added benefit. The classic meta-analysis on this controversy, an independent study from 2014, found:

GM Crops Can Help Feed the World's Growing Population

The *Boston Globe* recently published an article about community initiatives to combat food waste:

After years of encouraging residents to recycle their paper, plastic, bottles, and cans, more cities and towns are turning their attention to the next boulder in the waste stream: leftover food.

State environmental officials said there is a growing interest in creating residential programs for composting or food waste diversion since commercial restrictions went into effect in 2014.

The article also points to new and innovative opportunities to help fight this crisis, such as in schools:

[Marybeth] Martello said the next challenge is collecting food waste in the schools that is not edible and keeping that from the landfill. She said a pilot program is in the works and could launch in the fall.

In response to the article, Janet Carpenter penned the following commentary underscoring the importance of one critical tool not

On average, GM technology adoption has reduced chemical pesticide use by 37%, increased crop yields by 22%, and increased farmer profits by 68%. Yield gains and pesticide reductions are larger for insect-resistant crops than for herbicide-tolerant crops. Yield and profit gains are higher in developing countries than in developed countries.

In contrast, the farming methods advocated by Green America, EWG and other anti-GMO advocacy groups require more land, according to a 2018 study, published in Nature. Summing up the findings, study co-author, University of Sheffield researcher David Edwards:

mentioned that also has the potential to help address food waste: GMOs.

As your recent article suggests, community-wide efforts to reduce food waste and address hunger are critical to reducing the negative environmental impacts of our food systems and increasing access to adequate nutrition. That's important now and will become even more so in the future with projected population increases that will only stress this already fragile system more. One way to help address a coming food crisis on a global scale is genetically modified crops and the seeds for addressing this crisis are best planted now.

GM crops have already increased yields and reduced the environmental impact of farming, where they have been deployed, especially in developing countries where hunger is more prevalent. However, there is much unrealized potential for available GMO technologies that could be beneficial in countries where they are not currently grown, as well as from technology that is still in development.

The genetic modification of crops, with traits such as pest and disease tolerance, stress tolerance and enhanced nutritional characteristics can contribute to meeting the challenge of feeding the world's growing population in the decades to come.

"Responding to the Issue of Food Waste," Council for Biotechnology Information, August 21, 2018.

Organic [farming] systems are often considered to be far more environmentally friendly than conventional farming, but our work suggested the opposite. By using more land to produce the same yield, organic may ultimately accrue larger environmental costs.

Biotechnology critics maintain that food insecurity is mostly a political and economic crisis. "Hunger is the result of distribution and infrastructure problems, and it won't be eliminated by growing …. GMOs," organic advocacy group Just Label It writes on its website.

That's simplistic, maintains the World Health Organization (WHO). It says improving infrastructure is only one step on the way to establishing food security. As the Organization for Economic Co-Operation and Development (OECD) explains, yield-boosting biotech crops have been widely adopted in many parts of the developing world, though infrastructure in these countries is still lacking. The WHO agrees, pointing out that developing a "sustainable variety of crops" is also needed to address world hunger.

Building better infrastructure to distribute food is an important food security issue but only indirectly related to the controversy over the pros and cons of crop biotechnology. The economic growth that will finance investment in infrastructure is underway in many developing countries, but the climb out of poverty is still slow and uncertain.

According to the World Bank, market reforms cut the "1990 poverty rate in half by 2010." But gradual economic growth and agroecology aren't viable solutions for developing countries where food demands are growing dramatically, and their farmers whose crops are threatened by pests.

The Takeaway

Critics of crop biotechnology misrepresent the evidence that shows that GMOs can help developing countries combat hunger in numerous, specific ways. No, they will not "feed the world" by themselves, as GMO critics disingenuously claim. But as Calestous Juma, the late Harvard University professor of international development explained in 2017, planting genetically engineered crops is one of several important steps toward increasing food security in developing countries as they build their economies.
"African countries …. that have increased their food production …. relied on a system wide approach …. The measures include investing in rural infrastructure, improving technical training of farmers, leveraging new technologies, upgrading food processing and expanding local market access …. African leaders recognize that they can hardly grow their economies without raising agricultural productivity."

> *"The economic incentive to develop the sort of GM crops that would help small, poor farmers in third world nations is small since the financial returns would be modest."*

GMOs Can Feed the World, but We Need to Develop the Right Crops

Paul Diehl

In the following viewpoint, Paul Diehl gets straight to his point: GMOs can feed the world. However, he also argues that the promise of genetically modified foods is being missed. This is because, he claims, the countries that most desperately need these technologies have erected regulatory barriers preventing their adoption. Paul Diehl is a San Francisco-area biotech consultant.

As you read, consider the following questions:

1. Why is there little economic incentive to develop GM crops that would help farmers in developing nations, according to the author?
2. How does this viewpoint address the issue of large companies having a monopoly on GM foods?
3. What does the author say is one of the reasons for lessening resistance to GMOs?

"How GMOs Can Feed the World," by Paul Diehl, Dotdash Publishing Family, December 23, 2018. Reprinted by permission.

GM crop planting has experienced growth every year since 1996. In 2018, a record of 191.7 million hectares of biotech crops was planted—12% of the planet's arable land.

The growth of biotech crops is the fastest-growing segment in agriculture. While much of these crops are used for animal feed and biofuel, much of it also makes its way directly into the majority of processed foods sold in America and Asia.

One of the main benefits that advocates of genetically modified (GMO) foods have promoted is the ability of the technology to help alleviate world hunger. However, despite the success of GM crops, the technology is failing to deliver on the promise of food security worldwide.

The Drivers of the GM Food Revolution

Cost, profit, and crop yield are the driving factors behind GMOs. The first GMO food, the Flavr-Savr Tomato, reduced the cost to produce canned tomato products by about 20%, while numerous studies demonstrated the economic benefit for farmers who plant GMO crops.

Faster growth rates resulting in cheaper fish production is the main benefit touted for the AquaBounty salmon that became the first genetically modified (GM) animal approved to be sold as food.

It's clear that genetically engineered traits make plants and animals more resistant to disease. They stay ripe longer and grow more robustly in a variety of conditions. GMs are also effective in reducing costs, providing financial benefits for consumers and businesses alike.

Large agriculture companies that produce GM crops such as Monsanto, DuPont, and Syngenta generate large profits. Opportunities for smaller start-up biotech companies, such as AquaBounty and Arctic Apples abound.

Using GM Crops to Feed More People

Reduced costs, increased crop yield, rising profits, and more business opportunities are driving the growth of GM foods. The next logical step would be to use GM food to solve food insecurities. The advantages of using GM crops to reduce world hunger are plentiful, but anti-GM food sentiments abound as well.

Recent results of studies have demonstrated that the idea of curing hunger through GM plants is not panning out as anticipated. The countries that could benefit the most from genetic engineering have benefited the least.

There are many reasons for this resistance to the adoption of GMOs around the world.

Politics vs. Research and Distribution

Much of the inability of GM technology to provide relief for the poorest nations seems to have less to do with the technology and more with social and political issues. Many of the poorest countries most strongly affected by famine have set up onerous regulations that prevent the growth and import of GM food and crops.

Much of this resistance seems to have been prompted by groups in the past. There is still resistance to the adoption of GMOs, but increased rates of hunger around the world are influencing people to change their minds. European Union member countries are able to decide for themselves whether they want to adopt the technology.

Lack of information about the long-term consequences of GM foods leads many to believe that people should not be eating them. This reason does seem to have the most merit in all of the reasons for resisting food changes.

The resistance caused by social pressures and political positioning causes hunger research groups that focus on the development of crops and farming techniques to avoid GM plants.

The anti-GM sentiment, though, is not the only reason the technology has failed to benefit the poorest nations. Commercially, major crop development companies use genetic engineering primarily to improve large cash crops with the most potential for profits, such as corn, cotton, soy, and wheat.

Little investment is put into crops, such as cassava, sorghum, or millet which are more relevant for cultivation in poor nations. The economic incentive to develop the sort of GM crops that would help small, poor farmers in third world nations is small since the financial returns would be modest.

Using Genetic Engineering to Help Solve World Hunger

Big agricultural companies, farmers, and food producers have benefited the most from GM crops. The incentive of profits has certainly been helping move the development of the technology forward.

Some might even say that this the way things are supposed to work, with capitalism driving innovation. However, profit-driven efforts don't negate the possibility that the technology can also be applied to benefit society at large by reducing world hunger.

The fact remains that genetic engineering is a powerful tool for improving food production. There is no faster way to produce animals and plants with specific beneficial traits and, as we learn more about genetics, many more modifications will become possible.

Financial Motivations Must Be Overcome to Succeed

There is no question of whether to apply genetic engineering toward improving crops for food consumption. Genetic modification is already part of the crop improvement toolbox.

The real question to ask then is if, in addition to helping make many people wealthier in industrialized areas, this advanced technology will provide a solution to alleviate hunger in the poorest regions of the world.

Applying this technology to effectively solve the problems of world hunger would require reasonable engagement and coordination from a variety of corporations, political entities, and social groups. The benefits of GM food adoption will have to outweigh the financial gains or losses incurred.

Periodical and Internet Sources Bibliography

The following articles have been selected to supplement the diverse views presented in this chapter.

Kevin Bonham, "GMOs Are Still the Best Bet for Feeding the World," *Scientific American*, 31 March 2015. https://blogs. scientificamerican.com/food-matters/gmos-are-still-the-best-bet-for-feeding-the-world/

Maggie Caldwell, "Five Surprising Genetically Modified Foods," *Mother Jones*, 5 August 2016 https://www.motherjones.com/environment/2013/08/what-are-gmos-and-why-should-i-care/

Lorraine Chow, "GMOS Will Not Feed the World, New Report Concludes," EcoWatch, 31 May 2015. https://www.ecowatch.com/gmos-will-not-feed-the-world-new-report-concludes-1882023777.html

Nathanael Johnson, "So Can We Really Feed the World?—Yes, and Here's How," Grist, 10 February 2015. https://grist.org/food/so-can-we-really-feed-the-world-yes-and-heres-how/

Erik Kobaushi-Solomon, "This Company's GMOs Will Help Feed The World, Without Ever Being Eaten," Forbes.com, 31 May 2019. https://www.forbes.com/sites/erikkobayashisolomon/2019/05/31/this-companys-gmos-will-help-feed-the-world-without-ever-being-eaten/#6e1f6c215cc6

Eric Niiler, "Why Gene Editing Is the Next Food Revolution," *National Geographic*, 10 August 2018. https://www.nationalgeographic.com/environment/future-of-food/food-technology-gene-editing/

Tom Parrett, "GMO Scientists Could Save the World From Hunger, If We Let Them," *Newsweek*, 21 May 2015. https://www.newsweek.com/2015/05/29/gmo-scientists-could-save-world-hunger-if-we-let-them-334119.html

Brad Plumer, "Are Genetically Modified Foods Necessary to Feed the World?" Vox, 22 July 2015. https://www.vox.com/2014/11/3/18092774/are-genetically-modified-foods-necessary-to-feed-the-world

OPPOSING
VIEWPOINTS®
SERIES

CHAPTER 4

Is Increased Corporate Control of the Food System a Dangerous Idea?

Chapter Preface

The most commonly discussed potential problems of genetically modified foods are the dangers to the environment or to the health of individuals who consume these foods. However, there is another potential problem that is more difficult to categorize.

The problem was hinted at in the viewpoint by Million Belay in Chapter Three, in which he argues that African farmers do not need GMOs to feed their nation. His main point was that these farmers already had what they needed to grow food. However, he also suggested that these farmers were threatened not only by climate change and political realties, but also by the control of their seeds and crops by large multinational biotech companies.

In this chapter, the viewpoint authors address the role of big agro-tech head-on. In some viewpoints, the authors deny any benefit to genetically modified crops and say that the production and promotion of them is just a means for making profits rather than helping to feed the world. Others accept that GM crops may have some advantages. They may be able to save lives and feed the hungry. However, the greed of corporations is preventing that technology from helping those who most need the help. One viewpoint tells the story of a plant researcher who is taking an unusual and somewhat subversive approach to getting seeds back into the hands of farmers.

In the midst of it all, a Q&A with an expert in the economics of agriculture offers some insight into how and why agriculture is getting so big and consolidated—and why that is not likely to change any time soon.

> *"The real point behind Gmos is to achieve corporate / big government control of all agriculture, the biggest by far of all human endeavours. And this agriculture will be geared not to general wellbeing but to the maximization of wealth."*

Corporate Control of Farming Is the Real Point of GM Food

Colin Tudge

In the following viewpoint, Colin Tudge opens by arguing that Golden Rice is not necessary or even particularly good at providing vitamin A to the millions of people who need it. After explaining why, the author states that he believes genetically modified foods are not the answer to putting more nutritious food into the mouths of the malnourished. He goes on to say why so many governments and thought leaders argue so strongly that GM food is the answer. To really understand the issue, he says, you must "follow the money." Colin Tudge is a British biologist and science writer.

"The Real Point of GM Food Is Corporate Control of Farming," by Colin Tudge, The Ecologist, November 1, 2013. Reprinted by permission.

As you read, consider the following questions:

1. How, according to the author, has monocultural big-scale agriculture created the problem Golden Rice is supposed to solve?
2. How might well-planned cities help solve the problem of food insecurity and lack of necessary vitamins, according to the viewpoint?
3. What does author say is the "real purpose" of GM food? If true, why would this be alarming?

Governments these days are not content with agriculture that merely provides good food. In line with the dogma of neoliberalism they want it to contribute as much wealth as any other industry towards the grand goal of "economic growth."

High tech offers to reconcile the two ambitions—producing allegedly fabulous yields, which seems to be what's needed, and becoming highly profitable. The high-tech flavour of the decade is genetic engineering, supplying custom-built crops and livestock as GMOs (Genetically Modified Organisms).

The Myth of Golden Rice

So it was that the UK Secretary of State for the Environment and Rural Affairs, Owen Paterson, told The Independent recently that the world absolutely needs genetically-engineered "Golden Rice," as created by one of the world's two biotech giants, Syngenta. Indeed, those who oppose Golden Rice are "wicked": a comment so outrageous that Paterson's own civil servants have distanced themselves from it.

Specifically, Golden Rice has been fitted with genes that produce carotene, which is the precursor of vitamin A. Worldwide, approximately 5 million pre-school aged children and 10 million pregnant women suffer significant Vitamin A deficiency sufficiently severe to cause night blindness according to the WHO. By such statistics a vitamin A-rich rice seems eminently justified.

Yet the case for Golden Rice is pure hype. For Golden Rice is not particularly rich in carotene and in any case, rice is not, and never will be, the best way to deliver it. Carotene is one of the commonest organic molecules in nature. It is the yellow pigment that accompanies chlorophyll in all dark green leaves (the many different kinds known as "spinach" are a great source) and is clearly on show in yellow roots such as carrots and some varieties of cassava, and in fruits like papaya and mangoes that in the tropics can grow like weeds.

So the best way by far to supply carotene (and thus vitamin A) is by horticulture—which traditionally was at the core of all agriculture. Vitamin A deficiency is now a huge and horrible issue primarily because horticulture has been squeezed out by monocultural big-scale agriculture—the kind that produces nothing but rice or wheat or maize as far as the eye can see; and by insouciant urbanization that leaves no room for gardens.

Well-planned cities could always be self-sufficient in fruit and veg. Golden Rice is not the answer to the world's vitamin A problem. As a scion of monocultural agriculture, it is part of the cause. Syngenta's promotion of it is yet one more exercise in top-down control and commercial PR. Paterson's blatant promotion of it is at best naïve.

For Golden Rice serves primarily as a flagship for GMOs and GMOs are very big business—duly supported at huge public expense by successive governments. It is now the lynch-pin of agricultural research almost everywhere. The UK's Agriculture and Food Research Council of the 1990s even had the words "agriculture" and "food" air-brushed out to become the Biotechnology and Biological Research Council (BBSRC).

The Real Purpose of GM Food

We have been told that GMOs increase yields with lower inputs and have been proven beyond reasonable doubt to be safe. Indeed, journalist Mark Lynas has been telling us from some remarkably high platforms that the debate on GMOs is "dead"; that there is now "a consensus" among scientists worldwide that they are necessary and safe.

In reality, GMOs do not consistently or even usually yield well under field conditions; they do not necessarily lead to reduction in chemical inputs, and have often led to increases. And contra Mark Lynas, there is no worldwide consensus of scientists vouching for their safety.

Indeed, the European Network of Scientists for Social and Environmental Responsibility (ENSSER) has drawn up a petition that specifically denies any such consensus and points out that "a list of several hundred studies does not show GM food safety." Hundreds of scientists are expected to sign.

Overall, after 30 years of concerted endeavour, ultimately at our expense and with the neglect of matters far more pressing, no GMO food crop has ever solved a problem that really needs solving that could not have been solved by conventional means in the same time and at less cost.

The real point behind GMOs is to achieve corporate / big government control of all agriculture, the biggest by far of all human endeavours. And this agriculture will be geared not to general wellbeing but to the maximization of wealth.

The last hundred years, in which agriculture has been industrialised, have laid the foundations. GMOs, for the agro-industrialists, can finish the job. The technology itself is esoteric so that only the specialist and well-endowed can embark on it —the bigger the better.

All of the technology can be, and is, readily protected by patents. Crops that are not protected by patents are being made illegal. Only parts of the EU have so far been pro-GM but even so the list of crops that it allows farmers to grow—or any of us!—becomes more and more restricted. Those who dare to sell the seed of traditional varieties that have not been officially approved can go to prison. Your heritage allotment could soon land you in deep trouble.

The Upside of GMOs

The controversy surrounding genetically modified organisms is very heated and often political. If one were to believe all the naysayers, GMOs will leave all but the richest few humans dying of starvation in a matter of a decade. As any savvy consumer knows, however, there are two sides to every story. There are plenty of good reasons for the investment of time and money into GMOs.

What Is Genetic Modification?

Genetic modification is the science of replacing or adding genes from one organism to another to produce a beneficial result. Unlike selective breeding, which uses organisms that are very similar, genetic modification can use rather disparate plants and animals to get results. One example involves scientists who inserted daffodil and bacterial DNA into rice to give it a higher beta-carotene content. Daffodils and bacteria could never be cross-pollinated with rice using traditional breeding methods.

Benefits to Producers

GMOs can have many benefits for food producers. Plants can be designed to be insect-resistant, heartier or to grow under more extreme conditions. Animals can be modified to give more meat or milk, or to grow faster. This results in higher yields for farmers and

As GMOs spread—and governments like Britain's would love to follow the US lead in this—they could soon become the only options; the only kids on the block. Then all of agriculture, the key to human survival, will become the exclusive property of the few huge companies that hold the patents.

By every sane judgment this is a horrible prospect. Among many other things, the obvious loss of biodiversity will make the whole world even more precarious than it is right now, especially if climate changes the growing conditions year by year. Yet our government's support for GM technology and for the thinking better products. One example is slow-ripening tomatoes, which can be stored longer, hold up better to transportation and still provide superior taste and texture for consumers and manufacturers.

Benefits to Humans

In places where food is scarce or difficult to grow, plants and animals can be modified to provide more nutrients and grow better under harsh conditions. Scientists have added vitamins and minerals to staples like rice and corn to fight malnourishment in underdeveloped countries. Plants are more drought-resistant and easier to grow. Many plants are designed to use less pesticides and chemicals to grow, which means less exposure to these potentially toxic substances for farmers and consumers.

Benefits to the Environment

Many GMOs are tailored for specific environmental conditions, which means saving water in drought-prone areas and less use of chemicals. Higher yields and more efficient growth mean that the same amount of food is produced on less land, using fewer natural resources. Plants and animals become resistant to certain environmentally specific pathogens and insects, which reduces the chance of losing a crop to disease.

"What Are the Positives of GMO?" by Nola Moore, Leaf Group Ltd., September 26, 2017.

behind it is unswerving. Government wants agriculture to be seen as big business.

Lip service is still paid to democracy (young men and women are sent to their deaths to defend the idea of it) but in truth we have rule by oligarchy: a virtual coalition of corporates and government, with establishment scientists in attendance. This monolith, and the crude thinking on which it is founded, is a far bigger threat to humanity than North Korea or "terrorism," or the collapse of banks, or dwindling oil.

There Is No Alternative?

Yet we have been assured, time and again, that there is no alternative: that without high tech, industrialized agriculture, we will all starve. This is the greatest untruth of all; though it has been repeated so often by so many people in such high places that it has become embedded in the zeitgeist.

Whether the officially sanctioned untruths spring from misconception or from downright lies I will leave others to judge. But in either case, their repetition by people who have influence in public affairs, is deeply reprehensible.

Specifically we have been told that the world will need 50% more food by 2050. The Chief Scientific Adviser to the Government, Sir John Beddington, said this in his "Foresight" report of 2012 on The Future of Food and Farming.[1]

His argument was, and is, that a billion out of the present seven billion are now undernourished; that numbers are due to rise to 9.5 billion by 2050; that people "demand" more and more meat as they grow richer; and that meat requires enormous resources to produce (already the world's livestock gobble up about 50% of the world's cereal and well over 90% of the soya).

So of course we need 50% more—and some have raised the ante to 100%. Thus the message comes from on high, we must focus on production, come what may.

But others, including some far closer to the facts, tell a quite different story. Professor Hans Herren, President of the Millennium Institute in Washington, points out that the world already produces enough staple food to support 14 billion—twice the present number.

A billion starve because the wrong food is produced in the wrong places by the wrong means by the wrong people—and once the food is produced, as the Food and Agriculture Organization of the UN (FAO) has pointed out, half of it is wasted.

The UN demographers tell us that although human numbers are rising the percentage rise is going down and should reach zero by 2050—so the numbers should level out. Nine and a half billion is as many as we will ever have to feed, and we already produce 50% more than will ever be needed.

The task, then, is not to increase output, but to produce what we do produce (or even less) by means that are kinder to people, livestock, and wildlife; more sustainable; and more resilient.

The truth is that for commercial purposes—for the maximization of wealth—it is too easy to provide good food for everyone. A few years ago, after all, when the economy was tweaked a little differently, farmers in Europe and the US were embarrassed by gluts of wheat and maize; and as farmers have always known, gluts are second only to total crop failure as the route to financial disaster.

The obvious and sensible solution would be to reduce production: to tailor output to need and to genuine desire. "Set-aside" was a crude stab at this. But the far more lucrative course is the one we have taken: to overproduce.

And if it turns out that people really don't need more food, then those who seek primarily to maximize wealth must pretend that they do. So the word is put around, backed by well-chosen and uncritical statistics, that we will need 50% more in the next few decades.

The resulting surpluses are then fed to livestock. Livestock that could, incidentally, be fed in more than adequate numbers if we made better use of the world's grasslands, which account for about two-thirds of all agricultural land. Or—which is a straightforward scam, though again it can be made to look respectable—the surplus wheat and maize can simply be burnt if labelled "biofuel."

"Demand" (in this scenario) is judged not by what people actually say they want (who ever said they wanted wheat-based biofuel, or cereal-fed beef rather than grass-fed beef?) but by what can be sold by aggressive PR and successfully lobbied through complaisant government.

Then we are told that the 50% increase we are said to need can be provided only by industrial agriculture and that this industry, like all human endeavour, works most efficiently when driven by the maximally competitive global market. The pious slogan that is meant to justify all this is "sustainable intensification": more and more output per hectare, achieved by high tech. The magic bullet of GMOs is just part of the hype.

For if we really did need more food (and it would be good to produce more in some places) then the industrial high tech route is not the one to go down. As the IAASTD report[2] of 2009 pointed out (this being one of the few official reports of recent years that is truly worthwhile) the industrial farming that is supposed to be feeding the world in practice provides only 30% of the world's food.

Another 20% comes from fishing, hunting, and people's back gardens. The remaining 50% comes from the mostly small, mostly mixed traditional farms that the industrialists and their political assistants tell us are an anachronism. And small mixed farms can be the most productive of all, per unit area.[3]

Furthermore, to produce their 30%, the industrial farms gobble up enormous quantities of oil for their industrial chemistry with immense collateral damage, not least to the climate. In contrast traditional farms are low input, and at least when properly managed, need not be damaging at all.

More yet: traditional farms worldwide typically produce only about a half or even a third of what they could produce. Not because the farmers are incompetent, as Western observers like to claim, but because they lack the most basic supports.

For instance, if farm prices are left to the global market, they go up and down, and farmers who have no proper financial support from banks or governments are subjected to dumping of foreign surpluses.

They then cannot afford to invest upfront in more production. So they err on the side of caution, while subsidy-backed western industrial farmers, or at least the richest ones, have often thrown caution to the winds.

A little logistic help could double the output of traditional farms—50% of the whole. Heroic efforts would be needed to increase the output of high-tech western crops and livestock even by another 10%, because the 10-tonne per hectare wheat fields and the 10,000 litre-plus dairy cows are already hard up against physiological limits (while the livestock is well beyond welfare limits).

Yet all the official effort, and our money, is poured into more industrialization. Policy, agricultural and alas scientific, goes where the money leads.

Follow the Money

Finally, we are told that the high-tech, global market approach to food production keeps prices down. Small, mixed, traditional-style farms are said to be far too expensive because they are labour-intensive.

But in fact, about 80% of what people spend on food in supermarkets goes to the middle-men and the banks (who lend the money to set up the system in the first place). So the farmers get only 20%. If those farmers are up to their ears in debt, as they are likely to be if they have gone down the industrial high-tech route, then a fair slice of that 20% goes to the banks.

At most, the farm labour costs that we are supposed to try so hard to keep down probably account for less than 10% of the total food bill. It's the 80% we need to get down.

When farmers sell directly to customers they get 100% of the retail price. At farmers' markets they typically get around 70%; and through local shops at least 30%. With different marketing the small farmers can certainly make a good living—and farming as a whole in Britain could easily soak up all the million under-25s who are presently being invited to wile away their days in the job centre. (But then, agricultural economists don't tend to take social costs into account).

In short, agriculture in Britain and the world at large needs a sea-change—an "Agrarian Renaissance": different ways of farming and marketing and—most emphatically—different people in charge.

The oligarchy of corporates, government, and compliant academics has failed. Farming that can actually feed us is innately democratic. Worldwide, the farmers know best; but the oligarchs rarely talk to them. They are content merely to impose their scientific and economic and scientific dogmas: high tech in a neoliberal market.

Mercifully, worldwide, many people are helping to bring the Renaissance into being. They range from setters-up of local farmers' markets to organizations like ENSSER to the worldwide peasants' movement, La Via Campesina.

As many as can be fitted in congregate each year at the Oxford Real Farming Conference: the next one is in January 2014. Do come, and join the Renaissance. This is the cause of our age, for whatever else we may aspire to do, agriculture is the thing we absolutely have to get right.

Endnotes

1. Foresight. The Future of Food and Farming, GO-Science, 2011

2. International Assessment of Agricultural Knowledge, Science and Technology for Development (IAASTD), Island Press, 2009.

3. See for example Commentary IX (UNCTAD TER 2013): Comparative analysis of organic and non-organic farming systems: a critical assessment of on-farm profitability, Noemi Nemes, FAO

> "*[Bayer-Monsanto] will effectively control nearly 60% of the world's supply of proprietary seeds, 70% of the chemicals and pesticides used to grow food, and most of the world's GM crop genetic traits, as well as much of the data about what farmers grow where, and the yields they get.*"

Real People, Not Faceless Multinationals, Should Feed the World

John Vidal

In the following viewpoint, John Vidal discusses the merger of Monsanto and Bayer, two multinational companies—one in the agricultural sector, the other in chemicals and pharmaceuticals. The new company is known as Bayer. This move further consolidated the corporate control of agriculture. The author points out that this is just one in a series of corporate mergers that contributed to consolidating the food supply in the hands of multinational corporations. He goes on to share the story of a plant scientist who is trying to give farmers what they need to resist this control. John Vidal is a journalist and former environment editor of the Guardian.

As you read, consider the following questions:

1. The author points out that with the merger, Bayer will control "much of the data about what farmers grow where and the yields they get." Why does he think this is a problem?
2. Why was there so little opposition to the merger, according to the viewpoint?
3. Who is Debal Deb, and what is he doing to resist this trend?

U nless there is a major hiccup in the next few days, an incredibly powerful company will shortly be given a licence to dominate world farming. Following a nod from Donald Trump, powerful lobbying in Europe and a lot of political arm-twisting on several continents, the path has been cleared for Monsanto, the world's largest seed company, to be taken over by Bayer, the second-largest pesticide group, for an estimated $66bn (£50bn).

The merger has been called both a "marriage made in hell" and "an important development for food security." Through its many subsidiary companies and research arms, Bayer-Monsanto will have an indirect impact on every consumer and a direct one on most farmers in Britain, the EU and the US. It will effectively control nearly 60% of the world's supply of proprietary seeds, 70% of the chemicals and pesticides used to grow food, and most of the world's GM crop genetic traits, as well as much of the data about what farmers grow where, and the yields they get.

It will be able to influence what and how most of the world's food is grown, affecting the price and the method it is grown by. But the takeover is just the last of a trio of huge seed and pesticide company mergers. Backed by governments, and enabled by world trade rules and intellectual property laws, Bayer-Monsanto, Dow-DuPont and ChemChina-Syngenta have been allowed to control much of the world's supply of seeds. You might think that these mergers would alert the government, but because political parties in Britain are so inward-looking, and because most farmers in rich countries already buy their seeds from the multinationals, opposition has barely been heard.

Instead, it is coming from the likes of Debal Deb, an Indian plant researcher who grows forgotten crops and is the antithesis of Bayer and Monsanto. While they concentrate on developing a small number of blockbuster staple crops, Deb grows as many crops as he can and gives the seeds away.

This year he is cultivating an astonishing 1,340 traditional varieties of Indian "folk" rice on land donated to him in West Bengal. More than 7,000 farmers in six states will be given the seeds, on the condition that they also grow them and give some away.

This seed-sharing of "landraces," or local varieties, is not philanthropy but the extension of an age-old system of mutualised farming that has provided social stability and dietary diversity for millions of people. By continually selecting, crossbreeding and then exchanging their seeds, farmers have developed varieties for their aroma, taste, colour, medicinal properties and resistance to pests, drought and flood.

Deb's community seed bank is one of the last living repositories of hundreds of Indian rice varieties. It is also an act of ecological and political defiance against the immense reach and concentration of the likes of Monsanto and Bayer.

The corporates argue that only consolidation can bring the development of better seed varieties and the innovations needed to avert global hunger and malnutrition, as the world population climbs to around 10 billion people in a few decades' time.

By innovation, they mean new, "advanced" plant engineering technologies such as GM, Crispr, gene editing and bio-fortification. History, however, suggests strongly that the reality will be the opposite. It is far more likely, say environmentalists and farm groups in developing countries, that competition will be limited and that the legal and biological grip of seed corporates on global farming will tighten. The small farmer, who has traditionally fed the world and given societies their rich food cultures, will only be threatened further.

Forty years ago, farmers and consumer groups might have welcomed potential opportunities offered by agri-science and large corporate mergers. But today, there is no sense of agri-optimism. Yields of most staple crops have barely increased in years, seeds and herbicides are becoming more expensive, and the promised health, safety and nutritional benefits of new industrial crops have failed to materialise.

Instead, farm pollution increases, agricultural biodiversity continues to be lost and nearly 30 years and many billions of dollars of R&D after Monsanto breezed into Europe pledging to feed the world, there are still around 800 million people who are malnourished, no public enthusiasm for industrial farming, and open cynicism about corporate motives.

The UK and US governments, together with a few major agri-philanthropists such as the Gates Foundation, still plough billions of dollars a year into hi-tech, high-input farming, but the tide may be turning as simpler, grassroots solutions are being developed.

Nearly 10 million of the poorest farmers now use the system of rice intensification (SRI), which has been proven to increase rice, wheat, potato and other yields dramatically by stimulating the roots of crops. Agro-forestry techniques that grow trees and shrubs among crops is proving more productive, as is land restoration. Farmers' groups in India and across Latin America are developing their own seed companies in order to avoid the new corporate monopolies.

If they fail, the future of food appears to be in the hands of three giant companies that are wedded to genetic modification of one sort or another. The corporates might say that isn't a problem. Bayer's chairman, Werner Baumann, has recently promised to "strengthen its commitment in the area of sustainability," adding: "Agriculture is too important to allow ideological differences to bring progress to a standstill."

But still, blinded by the prospect of new technologies, governments and research organisations have paid little attention to farmers' traditional knowledge. They are missing out on this vast storehouse, which will be needed if the world is to adapt to climate change and population growth. Debal Deb, who lives on a shoestring and relies on friends for minimal funding to conduct his own research, has published research into rice varieties capable of growing in 12ft of water, others that can grow in 4-5ft of water, and dozens that are drought-tolerant, as well as many varieties that can grow in brackish water.

Some are said to be far richer in nutrients such as iron, zinc, magnesium, omega 3 and riboflavin than anything that the giant seed companies have developed. But such is the lack of trust and funds, Deb keeps the exact location of his farm secret and only gives his seeds to people he respects. He claims that spies have been sent to steal his seeds and companies want to patent, suppress or claim them as their own.

Instead of working in a well-funded research institute, as might be expected of a Fulbright biotech scholar, Deb is now part of the worldwide farmers' movement to limit corporate control and to redefine what knowledge is, and who owns it. Like many others, he has found that the best way to save traditional agricultural knowledge is to grow seeds and give them away. He believes that's the future. Pray that he's right.

> "Although transparency is not a
> cure-all, including people in the
> decision-making process and
> providing information about how an
> organization reached its decision can
> lead to greater decision acceptance."

Transparency in Labeling Laws Can Help Create Acceptance of GM Foods

Katherine McComas, Graham Dixon, and John C. Besley

In the following viewpoint, we turn back to questions of labeling for GM foods, but this time taking into account the perspective of large food companies. Katherine McComas, Graham Dixon, and John C. Besley look at what consumers expect from the large food companies that are increasingly in charge of the food supply. Katherine McComas is professor of communications at Cornell University. Graham Dixon is assistant professor of science risk communication at Washington State University. John C. Besley is associate professor of advertising and public relations at Michigan State University.

As you read, consider the following questions:

1. Why might large food manufacturers be willing to voluntarily label GM food products?
2. What was the industry's main argument against labelling laws?
3. Why is consumer involvement both useful and important, according to the viewpoint?

The fast-approaching July 1, 2016, deadline for Vermont's new labeling law—and a new federal proposal that would set a national system for disclosure—for genetically modified (GM) food has provoked a range of responses from food manufacturers while reigniting debate about the need to balance the weight of scientific evidence against consumer demand for transparency. At the center of the debate lay questions of trust in science and how the ways we communicate risk serve to increase or decrease that trust.

On the industry side, in January, Campbell declared support for mandatory labeling for products containing GM ingredients, and in March, General Mills announced its own intent to voluntarily label GM food products. Other big players, such as chocolatier Mars, have made similar announcements. With Vermont's labeling law looming, General Mills and others have appeared to focus their efforts on arguing for a nationwide approach to GM food labeling.

Perhaps not coincidentally, General Mills' announcement came only days after the failed efforts by the US House and some members of the US Senate to ban states from requiring mandatory GM food labeling. Specifically, the House bill would have prohibited states from requiring GM food labeling on the basis that informing them is not "necessary to protect public health and safety or to prevent the label from being false or misleading." The Senate bill sought to establish voluntary labeling standards for GM foods, an effort that ultimately expired due to lack of needed support.

As the debate over GM food labeling continues to rage, it's worth looking at the reasons consumers support or oppose labeling. A body of communication research, including a recent study we co-authored, suggests that consumers' views on GM foods reflect their values and how information about labeling is communicated to them more than the actual science.

Shouldn't Latest Science Settle It?

The fault lines over GM food labeling at this point are well-established.

On the one hand, labeling proponents argue that consumers have the right to know what is in the food they purchase so as to avoid possible health risks associated with GM ingredients. Others argue that labeling gives consumers the ability to avoid GM ingredients as a larger ideological statement about agro-food industry.

More generally, one could say that resistance to labeling flies against consumer demand in an age when experts admonish us to read nutrition labels to watch our sugar intake and avoid certain types of fats. Also, not telling people makes it look like there is something that the food manufacturers are hiding, which can damage the trust consumers place in them.

On the other hand, labeling opponents point to a lack of scientific evidence that GM ingredients are harmful to public health or the environment and argue that labeling will present an unnecessary financial burden on food manufacturers. Others note that consumers who wish to avoid food with GM ingredients already have the option to purchase organic food products, which provide non-GM options.

Regarding the balance of scientific evidence on safety, a recently released National Academies of Sciences (NAS) report would seem to lay to rest the issue. Its exhaustive review of over 900 scientific publications found, among other things, no solid findings showing a difference between the health risks of eating genetically engineered or conventionally bred food ingredients.

It is doubtful, however, that the NAS report will entirely remove public doubt about the risks or demands for labeling.

Research on public risk perceptions shows that it is not only the objective scientific assessment of risk that matters but also the subjective qualities of risk. These include whether people have control over their exposure to potential risks and whether they believe the risks are well-understood by scientists. Trust in the risk managers is also key, and people want to have a voice in decisions that ultimately affect them.

Value of Consumer Involvement

In terms of risk perceptions, results from a 2015 Pew Center study found that 57 percent of Americans did not believe that GM foods are safe. The Pew study found that 67 percent do not believe that scientists yet have a clear understanding of the public health implications of GM foods. Indeed, the Pew study found that the strongest predictor of believing that GM foods are safe is whether people believe scientists have a clear understanding of the risks.

In comparison, 88 percent of scientists with the American Association for the Advancement of Science (AAAS) believed GM foods to be safe.

Some may see this opinion divide as evidence of an irrational public. We see it as evidence of communication processes that have paid inadequate attention to how consumers' values affect risk-based decision making.

Rather than having a voice in the decisions, consumers are mostly asked to trust the experts, typically a faceless government institution or regulatory body. This can lead to a disconnect in what scientists and consumers consider the relevant facts in a decision.

Our own research, recently published in the Journal of Risk Research, found that people are much more supportive of a labeling decision (regardless of the outcome) when they were told that food companies had considered public input before making their decision. Therefore, recounting consumers' influence in GM labeling decisions is an important factor on how people support the decisions.

Examples show how some organizations are recognizing the importance of conveying this information. In the press release accompanying the recent NAS report, Committee Chair Fred Gould offered this statement: that the committee "focused on listening carefully and responding thoughtfully to members of the public who have concerns about GE crops and foods…."

Similarly, Campbell's President and Chief Executive Officer Denise Morrison said in a New York Times article about the food manufacturer's labeling decision, "We've always believed consumers have a right to know what's in their food…. We know that 92 percent of Americans support G.M.O. labeling, and transparency is a critical part of our purpose."

Examining the effect of these statements remain questions for future research. Our previous work would suggest, however, that underscoring how public input was considered may likely lead to greater support for the NAS conclusions or Campbell's decision, even if people do not wholly endorse the outcomes.

Although transparency is not a cure-all, including people in the decision-making process and providing information about how an organization reached its decision can lead to greater decision acceptance.

To this end, incorporating consumers' values in decisions that affect them, such as what ingredients manufacturers put in their food products, and communicating that back to the public can go a long way toward building trust and bridging the gaps between scientific and public understanding of risk.

> *"If we center the conversation on transparency and education instead of prescriptive policies, we put consumers in charge, not politics."*

Even If GMOs Are Safe, Mandatory Labeling Is a Good Idea

Mahni Ghorashi

In the following viewpoint, Mahni Ghorashi provides a succinct description of the debate about genetically modified foods. After briefly explaining the view of each side, the author argues that consumers have the right to know what they are eating. In addition, they have a responsibility to understand how economics influences the science behind these new foods. Mahni Ghorashi is co-founder of Clear Labs, a company in Menlo Park, California, that uses DNA testing to determine the content of commercially produced foods, looking particularly for the presence of certain pathogens.

"Even If GMOs Are Safe, Mandatory Labeling Is a Good Idea," by Mahni Ghorashi, Food Safety News, Marler Clark, March 24, 2016. Reprinted by permission. Article available at: https://www.foodsafetynews.com/2016/03/124802/

As you read, consider the following questions:

1. Why does the author say that we need GMO labelling even if the products are safe?
2. How are GMO labelling laws an advantage to the organic food industry?
3. The author argues that the public needs to be allowed to make a decision "free of political or business influences." Do you think that is likely to happen? Why or why not?

In November 2015 the FDA approved the first genetically engineered salmon as fit for human consumption, paving the way for genetically modified organisms to become a regular part of the American diet. The "super salmon" designed by AquaBounty Technologies produces growth hormones year round rather than just during the summer and reaches adult size in 18 months instead of three years. Not surprisingly, consumer and environmental groups have loudly opposed the FDA's decision—there's widespread unease when it comes to GMOs.

Regardless whether you think GMOs are safe or not, the United States needs a mandatory GMO labeling law. Consumers have the right to make purchasing decisions with confidence. If we want to support mandatory-labeling legislation, we've got to forge some some alliances that span the aisle of the GMO debate. Proponents of mandatory labeling need to be clear that they support transparency, not the outright banning of all GMOs. People have they right to know what they eat, but they also have a responsibility to understand how economic interests manipulate GMO politics.

If we center the conversation on transparency and education instead of prescriptive policies, we put consumers in charge, not politics. To move forward, we have to confront the fact that the GMO debate has been tainted, not only by politics and economic self-interest, but also by a pervasive cultural fear that technology threatens the perceived sanctity of nature.

The Costs and Benefits of GMOs

Proponents of GMO crops, including many large farmers and producers of them, are fighting against organic farmers, specialty retailers and major organic brands. They see mandatory labeling laws as an undue economic burden with little to no scientific bearing.

Meanwhile, the pro-labeling stance is held by the fast-growing organic food industry, which sees labeling as a competitive advantage. Proponents of GMOs contend that not a single conclusive test, credible report or any scientific data points to GMO crops being harmful to humans. They also point to the good that GMOs have done, reducing by a factor of 10 the amount of insecticides used on some crops, while simultaneously reducing food costs and decreasing CO_2 emissions. With nine billion people forecasted to populate the planet by 2050, the world will have to grow 70% more food by 2050 to keep pace with population growth.

Opponents of so-called Frankenfoods are equally militant. And they speak with their dollars. Non-GMO is one of fastest growing label trends in US food packages, with sales of items growing 28% last year to about $3 billion, according to a report in the *Wall Street Journal*. Many claim GMO crops are just a ploy by Monsanto, Bayer and Dupont to sell more herbicides, dominate the supply chain, and leave farmers solely dependent on high-priced transgenic seeds. They believe that inserting foreign genes into crops can make food dangerous or allergenic. The truth lies somewhere in between.

A (Very) Brief History of Genetic Engineering

Defenders of genetic engineering remind us that humans have been genetically modifying food for thousands of years via artificial selection, with large swaths of genes being swapped or altered in the breeding process, often unpredictably. Farmers were crossbreeding plants and animals to select for desirable characteristics long before the German monk Gregor Mendel began conducting his pea-plant experiments in the mid-19th century.

Today's genetic engineers can target single genes, making them perhaps the most efficient breeders the world has ever known. You'll find many them walking the halls of CalTech, Harvard and MIT, but genetic engineers congregate in far larger numbers in the waiting rooms of doctor's offices, elementary-school classrooms and subway cars—viruses, the world's first genetic engineers, have been inserting their DNA into genomes of crops and humans since the dawn of evolution, cross-pollinating the genes of other species. In fact, the humane genome is filled with genetic sequences originating in viruses.

The lesson here is that to determine whether a food item is "natural" or not, we rely on value judgements that are mostly personal. We ignore the fact that humans have been cross breeding plants and animals for millennia while we object to more precise, and most likely safer, forms of genetic engineering. Nature is never as pure as we wish it to be.

What We Can Learn from Science-Fiction

In referring to genetically modified food like super salmon as "Frankenfoods," opponents of GMOs explicitly allude to the world's first science-fiction novel, Mary Shelley's Frankenstein. They also betray the fact that the contentious GMO debate is largely motivated by two emotions: fascination and fear. Calling GMOs "Frankenfoods" is simply a catchy way of labeling them monstrous, unnatural things. Monsters, as any child knows, are both fascinating and frightful. Even more interesting is the fact that the term "Frankenfood" most accurately alludes to Shelley's character Victor Frankenstein, the scientist, not the unnamed monster he pieces together in a lab. Composed in the throes of the Industrial Revolution, Shelley's novel is a cautionary tale: Victor Frankenstein is a brilliant, lonely technologist who upsets the natural order in attempting to engineer a new species. Frankenstein attempts to play God, and he is punished for his pride.

Like Frankenstein and his "monster," genetic engineers and GMOs inspire intense negative emotions because they challenge

GMOs As a Corporate Control Tactic

When biotech companies like Monsanto, Dow, Dupont and Syngenta create GMO seeds, they're also creating entire systems of food production. By creating a suite of products designed to work together—seeds for crops engineered to withstand Roundup, a probably human carcinogen, for example—they're able to control the entire farming cycle and block out competition. Not only that, but the explosion of herbicide-resistant seeds has given way to herbicide-resistant weeds, fueling the growth of "superweeds" and ensuring that farmers must continue to buy increasingly harsh chemicals, often from the same company, to compensate.

Beyond this, seed options are slim. In 2009 in the United States, 93 percent of soybeans and 80 percent of corn were grown with seeds containing Monsanto-patented genetics.

Choice becomes increasingly illusory as mega-mergers become more common—Monsanto may soon merge with Bayer, and a Dow-Dupont merger was announced and remains on the table. (Agricultural chemical giant ChemChina is also in the process of acquiring Syngenta, for a cool $43 billion). And the dominance of GMOs makes things harder for those who go organic, since organic and non-GMO farmers have to spend time and money to prevent GMO contamination of their fields by crops from nearby farms.

Meanwhile, the power and influence of these huge corporations have spread beyond the agriculture industry to political campaigns and regulatory processes around the world. Mounting allegations of scientific censorship at the USDA point to the agency making decisions to appease companies like Monsanto. And in 2010, we found that top food and agricultural biotechnology interests spent more than half a billion dollars lobbying Congress between 1999 and 2009 and more than $22 million in campaign contributions.

Agrichemical heavyweights are spending millions to make it hard for us to know if GMOs are in our food. And if we don't know where our food is coming from, we don't know how little choice we have about what we eat—or what chemicals are being used to grow it.

"GMOs As a Corporate Control Tactic," by Kiley Fisher, Food & Water Watch, May 27, 2016.

our perception of what is natural. This is why GMO discourse so often devolves into a struggle between technology and nature, a false opposition that has been with us since before the Industrial Revolution and remains unresolved. When we pit technological innovation against the perceived sanctity of nature, we hijack proactive, constructive debate.

Mandatory Labeling

A *New York Times* survey found that 93% of Americans believe foods containing GMO ingredients should be labeled to reflect that. Increasingly, consumers are demanding assurance that food products are safe, for real-time information on purchases, and for product origination insight. Opponents of GMO labeling say it would be expensive and raise costs for consumers, but the reality is that 64 other countries have GMO labeling laws and food prices haven't increased. Consumers haven't stopped eating GMO foods. They simply have more information about what is in their food and how it's produced, which is how it should be.

More transparent labeling is also good for the top line— clear labels are a major factor in influencing consumer-purchase decisions when shopping for food or beverage products. The food industry is beginning to catch on. Campbell, General Mills, and Mars recently announced that they'll be labeling all GMO ingredients voluntarily. Vermont became the first US state to require mandatory labeling for foods containing GMOs starting in July of this year. Maine and Connecticut have also passed labeling laws, but those depend on neighboring states taking similar steps. In July 2015, Congress banned states from requiring mandatory GMO labeling. Perhaps unsurprisingly, the bill, called the Safe and Accurate Food Labeling Act of 2015, was backed by industry groups like Monsanto. Ultimately, a national standard for labeling laws is preferable to state standards.

Consumers need consistent, transparent, and recognizable labels. Some of us see distorted, dangerous monsters where others perceive deliciously plump salmon. When it comes to food, most of our purchasing decisions are rooted in emotions, personal values, and perception. Innovative new technologies are now dramatically illuminating product origin and quality insights. It's time we give consumers the information they deserve to make the best personal decisions, free of political or business influences.

> *"It is a sad irony that GMO technology is actually increasing food insecurity. This is based on the fact that under capitalism, agro-corporations have profit margins as their number one priority."*

GM Foods Serve Corporate Greed, Not Human Need

Ghiselle Karim

In the following viewpoint, Ghiselle Karim does not take issue with the safety of genetically modified foods and indeed begins by touting the potential advantages of the technology. GM foods could, she argues, help provide the world with more plentiful and nutritious food. Yet the huge corporations in charge of this technology have not used it to do so. Instead, they have used these technologies to enrich themselves at the expense of the poor and hungry. Ghiselle Karim wrote this viewpoint for Fightback, the Canadian section of the International Marxist Tendency.

"Genetically-Modified Food: For Human Need or Corporate Greed?" by Ghiselle Karim, Marxism.ca, October 9, 2013. Reprinted by permission.

As you read, consider the following questions:

1. What is the number one priority of agricultural corporations, according to the viewpoint?
2. What are "terminator seeds," and how do they keep power in the hands of agro-tech companies?
3. What solution does the author offer for protecting the food supply?

The development of genetically-modified organisms (GMO) has opened up whole new possibilities for improving the nutrition of humanity. For the first time, humans are able to genetically engineer species or organisms by transferring DNA between totally different organisms, potentially allowing for food to be grown in harsher climates, for example, or for existing crops to yield more food. However, under capitalism, GMOs are being abused by large agro-corporations, such as Monsanto, to maximize shareholders' profits at the expense of ordinary people around the world. Instead, GMOs have reduced the safety and security of the food system for billions of people. What is a working-class approach to confronting the problems of GMOs and food security?

According to the agricultural giant Monsanto, genetically engineered foods are produced to address issues of food insecurity and feed the world's booming population. But, if we look at the products being produced by companies like Monsanto, we find that this claim is evidently false. Companies like Monsanto have not come even remotely close to solving the question of hunger and lack of food. The United Nations' Food and Agriculture Organization (FAO) estimates that about 870-million people around the world (or, in other words, about one person out of every eight), suffered from chronic undernourishment in the period between 2010 and 2012. In fact, hunger kills more people every year than AIDS, malaria, and tuberculosis combined.

Despite the biotech industry's assurances, none of the genetically modified traits currently exhibited offer increased harvest, drought tolerance, enhanced nutrition, or any other consumer benefit. Moreover, GMO technology does not address the bigger reasons for why so many people go hungry, all of which are products of the capitalist system: poverty, lack of access to food, and a lack of access to land to grow it on.

It is a sad irony that GMO technology is actually increasing food insecurity. This is based on the fact that under capitalism, agro-corporations have profit margins as their number one priority. One such example is the fact that over 80% of all GMOs around the world are engineered for herbicide tolerance and, as a result, usage of toxic herbicides such as Monsanto's Roundup has increased by 15 times. GMO seeds are also responsible for the rise of "super weeds" and "super bugs" which can only be destroyed with ever more toxic poisons such as 2,4-D. Not surprisingly, the corporations that are pushing GMOs are the same ones who produce the chemical products that GMO crops rely upon. Monsanto has also inserted genes in its seeds that are resistant to their own advertised weed-killers, encouraging farmers to buy Monsanto chemicals and spray them over the crops with the knowledge that it will stay alive while other organisms competing for the soil's minerals will be eliminated. As well, genetically-engineered crops create super-pests and super-weeds as these organisms can adapt to the foreign gene and eventually become resistant to it.

In order to further increase profits at the expense of ordinary people, Monsanto creates seed sterilizing technology or "terminator" and "suicide seeds." These are plants which are genetically engineered to kill their own seeds. This means that seeds harvested from terminator crop will not germinate if planted the following season, which has been the basis of farming since the dawn of agriculture. The goal of this technology is clearly to exploit seed industry profits by preventing farmers from reusing seeds from their harvest and thus forcing them to purchase GM seeds from Monsanto's commercial seed market. Recently in Colombia, farmers have been forced to use GE seeds, if refused they would be imprisoned. In other words, by terminator genetic engineering method or sterilizing farm-saved seeds, farmers are forced to return to commercial seed market every year and this purposely created a cycle of dependency.

Because GMO is a new innovation, biotechnology corporations have obtained a patent which restricts their use to others or forbids others from further researching even their side effects. As a result, GMO creators now have the authority to sue farmers whose non-GM fields are cross-pollinated with GMOs, even when it occurs naturally. GMOs therefore pose a serious threat to farmer sovereignty and to the national food security of any country where they are grown. This monopolization had been affecting the farmer sovereignty (especially in developing countries) and the national food security wherever they are grown. According to environmental activist Vandana Shiva, the harsh reality of GMO innovation is that it leads to global famine and poverty as the seeds are controlled and patented by Monsanto.

Of course, none of these seeds or chemicals come cheaply for farmers. The actions by corporations such as Monsanto are further pushing more of the world's farmers into poverty and some are forced completely out of agricultural jobs.

Perhaps even worse is the fact that most farmers are being compelled to use this agricultural technology. Monsanto held secret test in India where genetically-engineered cotton was grown without farmers' awareness and no bio-safety measures were taken during these trials. Monsanto specifically chose India to hold its trials as there would be no issues to bribe the government and manipulate the subsistence farmers' need for cheap seed.

But, these practices are not just limited to the ex-colonial world. Even in Canada, farmers have had to face unjust pressure and marketing tactics from companies like Monsanto, Dow, AgraEvo, and Zeneca. For example, to promote the use of Bovine Growth Hormone (rBGH), these companies have hidden negative results of rBGH trials, refused to disclose their grants and donations to university clinics in the USA, and threatened Canadian scientists who, in their opinion, are holding up the approval of rBGH in Canada.

Aside from food security, there is also evidence that there are real health risks associated with the GMO industry, mainly to do with the heavy reliance on chemicals that these modified crops depend upon. Once again using one of Monsanto's products as an example, Roundup has been linked to elevated hormone levels in people. Although some alleged health risks around GMO may be exaggerated, it is also hard to trust the safety claims made by the agro-firms, themselves, considering the extent they have gone to push GMO technology on unsuspecting farmers and consumers.

Companies like Monsanto have used their financial muscle to get governments to go along with their pursuit for profit. In the USA, President Barack Obama earlier this year signed into law an agricultural bill that essentially guarantees agro-corporations the ability to continue selling and marketing GMO seeds, even if their safety is later called into question by the US Food & Drug Administration (USFDA). This goes to show that, under capitalism, a company's bottom line is put before our health and safety.

Socialism Is Needed to Protect Our Food

Not surprisingly, there has been a wave of protests against GMOs around the world as people try to protect their livelihoods and their source of sustenance. In India, genetically-modified fields of cotton have been burned; in Liverpool, there has been a boycott in the unloading of genetically-modified soybeans; and around the world, people have trampled sites where GM crops are being tested. This is a radicalized movement fighting back against the attempt to manipulate the global food market.

As socialists we are not opposed to GMO innovation as this biotechnology has incredible potential to benefit humanity in many ways if used correctly. Human insulin, for instance, has been grown in GM yeast for decades, improving and even saving the lives of many individuals with diabetes. However, as it is evident today under capitalism, ordinary working people have no control over how this technology is used. For instance, a socialist system would not ignore the clear side effects of herbicides such as Monsanto's Roundup on human health. The doubts that many people have of GMO technology is only natural given the extreme secrecy demonstrated by agro-corporations; under a socialist society, all information and results of GMO testing would be open to public scrutiny. With all the information available to the working class, we would then be able to weigh the advantages and disadvantages of the GMO foods and make an informed decision whether to pursue this technology or not.

Therefore, we demand the full worker and public control over all GMO production and research, and nationalization of big agribusiness to place control into the hands of the working class. We demand to end the patents on seeds as it is unjust and disadvantageous for the farmers. We demand further scientific research to prove that GMOs do not have negative side effects on human health, as giant Monsanto claims. We demand a clear labeling of all products that contain GM organisms so that people know what they are ingesting in their own bodies. Most importantly, we demand that it is our basic human right to protect our food supply.

Under socialism, all the giant food companies would be in the hands of the working class and its production would be planned to meet human need, not corporate greed. We have hunger not because there is not enough food, but rather because it it is not distributed equally. The core of the problem is not a shortage of food, but capitalism!

> *"GM crops are not the answer to this shameful global situation, but I argue strongly that they provide another tool, another option to try to address the problem."*

GM Crops Are a Valuable Tool in Addressing Global Poverty

Mark Tester

The previous viewpoint argued that capitalism and control of biotech by large corporations contributed to poverty. In the following viewpoint, Mark Tester sees things somewhat differently. He acknowledges that unequal distribution of food is a huge problem. However, he also points out that generating new plants that can respond well to climate challenges can be an important tool in solving the problems of poverty and hunger. Mark Tester is an Australian botanist and plant scientist.

As you read, consider the following questions:

1. Why is the salinity of soils increasing, and why is that a problem?
2. This author notes the problems of inequality of access to food, yet he sees GM crops as a necessary tool in addressing poverty. Is there a contradiction there?
3. Do you agree with the author that it is not important who funds the research discussed in this viewpoint or other similar research? Why or why not?

Salty soils affect the growth of plants worldwide, particularly in irrigated land where one-third of the world's food is produced. It is estimated that one-fifth of irrigated land is salt-affected. And it is a problem that is only going to get worse as pressure to use more water increases and the quality of water decreases. Helping plants to withstand this salty onslaught would have a significant impact on world food production.

Salt in the soil also affects dryland agriculture, particularly in semi-arid regions of the world, such as in the Middle East, Kazakhstan and Australia. 70% of Australia's wheat crop is affected by salt that is found as much a metre beneath the surface—this is important, as Australia is one of the world's largest exporters of wheat.

Any approaches which can be taken to reduce the impact of salinity on world food production would be valuable. The world food situation is now critical. More than one billion people now go hungry each day. World grain stores are now lower than they have been for fifty years, since before the Green Revolution. Reflecting this, prices have increased greatly. Pressures from increasing population, increasing standards of living and biofuels, all in the context of global climate change, are making demands that are increasingly difficult to meet.

The inequitable distribution of food is, of course, very important, as are problems of distribution of better seed varieties and basic farming technologies to farmers. These are perennial issues which intergovernmental organisations (such as the Consultative Group on International Agricultural Research) and charities (eg the Rockefeller Foundation) have battled valiantly to address for decades. And support for this must continue. But despite such wonderful work and many local victories, the problems globally are getting worse, not better. We need more and, perhaps, different strategies—including new technologies.

In my group's research over the past ten years, we have been studying the mechanisms plants use to tolerate salinity, and how to manipulate these processes so that plants can keep growing while the salt keeps rising.

We have generated plants that are much more tolerant to salt, work which was published yesterday.

One mechanism of salinity tolerance involves keeping the toxic sodium ion ($Na+$) out of the leaves. One way to do this is to reduce the amount of $Na+$ moving from the roots to the shoots in the stream of water that flows up through the plant's water conducting pipes.

We made a targeted genetic tweak so that $Na+$ is removed from the water flowing up the stem before it reaches the shoot—once out, it is stuck. The effect of this manipulation is to reduce the amount of toxic $Na+$ building up the shoot and so increase the plant's tolerance to salinity.

The control of the gene we manipulated is crucial. To be effective, it must be tuned up so that it works harder and produces more protein than it usually would specifically around the plant's water conducting tubes in the mature root. In doing this, we have enhanced a process used naturally by plants to minimise the movement of $Na+$ to the shoot. We have used genetic modification (GM) to amplify the process, helping plants to do what they already do—but to do it much better!

We are now in the process of transferring the technology to crops such as rice, wheat and barley. And results in rice already look very promising.

The motivation for my research is as an independent academic seeking knowledge and its application for public good. It is driven by the same imperatives that led me to be an active member of the UK Green party for nearly a decade. As such, I consider my funding sources to be irrelevant to my academic integrity. Nevertheless, I can declare that none of our research on salinity has been paid for by industry. All funding has been from UK, EU or Australian governmental sources or from charities such as the Leverhulme Foundation. Furthermore, the outputs described in the paper are fully and freely available for public benefit. I hope very much that the principles of our work can be applied to develop salt-tolerant crops in developing countries and give farmers on low-quality soils a better chance at improving their lot.

And giving people a chance to better their situation is something we need to facilitate, not impede. The west may not need more food, but remember Make Poverty History—a child dies unnecessarily as a result of extreme poverty every three seconds. GM crops are not the answer to this shameful global situation, but I argue strongly that they provide another tool, another option to try to address the problem. And I do not think those of us sitting in comfortable wealth have a right to deny people the opportunity to improve their production of food. The technology is just that, a technology. Like nuclear technologies (radiotherapy or nuclear weapons) or mobile phones (communication or bomb triggers), how we use it is the main issue. I hope that the plants we have generated provide a subtle use of GM technology that will allow some positive benefits for the developing world.

Periodical and Internet Sources Bibliography

The following articles have been selected to supplement the diverse views presented in this chapter.

Christopher D. Cook, "Control over Your Food: Why Monstanto's GM Seeds Are Undemocratic," *Christian Science Monitor*, 23 February 2011. https://www.csmonitor.com/Commentary/Opinion/2011/0223/Control-over-your-food-Why-Monsanto-s-GM-seeds-are-undemocratic

Lisa Cornish, "How Do Corporations Perceive Their Role in the GMO Debate?" Devex, 11 May 2018. https://www.devex.com/news/how-do-corporations-perceive-their-role-in-the-gmo-debate-92507

Caitlin Dewey, "The Government Is Going to Counter 'Misinformation' about GM Foods," *Washington Post*, 3 May 2017. https://www.washingtonpost.com/news/wonk/wp/2017/05/03/the-government-is-going-to-try-to-convince-you-to-like-gmo-foods/

Kiley Fisher, "GMOs as a Corporate Control Tactic," Common Dreams, 29 May 2016. https://www.commondreams.org/views/2016/05/29/gmos-corporate-control-tactic

Ann Hui, "What Happens When a Few Big Companies Control the World's Food Production?" *Globe and Mail*, 17 May 2018. https://www.theglobeandmail.com/news/national/agri-food-mergers-spark-concerns-over-seed-diversity/article31919856/

Dan Mitchell, "Why Monsanto Always Wins," *Fortune*, 26 June 2014. https://fortune.com/2014/06/26/monsanto-gmo-crops/

Richard Schiffman, "GMOs Aren't the Problem. Our Industrial Food System Is, *Guardian*, 6 November 2013. https://www.theguardian.com/commentisfree/2013/nov/06/genetically-modified-food-safe-monsanto

Carin Smaller, "Bayer Tightens Control over the World's Food Supply," International Institute for Sustainable Development, 23 September 2016. https://www.iisd.org/blog/bayer-tightens-control-over-world-s-food-supply

Hannah Steiner, "A Brief Explanation about GMOs Companies," Tired Earth, 16 February 2019.https://www.tiredearth.com/articles/brief-explanation-about-gmos-companies

Caroline Winter and Tom Loh, "With Each Roundup Verdict, Bayer's Monsanto Purchase Looks Worse," *Bloomberg Businessweek*, 18 September 2019. https://www.bloomberg.com/news/features/2019-09-19/bayer-s-monsanto-purchase-looks-worse-with-each-roundup-verdict

For Further Discussion

Chapter 1

1. In this chapter Jeffrey Smith outlines a talk he gave about GMOs and cancer. In this piece, he says that several cancer rates are rising "in parallel" with use of glyphosate on GM soy and corn crops. Does evidence that two things are increasing at the same time or rate prove that these increases are caused by the same thing? Why or why not? Do you notice a difference in the way the science is discussed in this viewpoint and the sidebar that follows it?

2. In the last viewpoint in this chapter, a website interviewed four experts about the safety of genetically modified foods. All insisted that such foods are safe. Would you have felt differently about the experts views had the panel included someone with a different perspective? Why or why not? How do you think these viewpoints compare to others you've read in this chapter?

Chapter 2

1. Several authors in this chapter have pointed out that crops can be genetically engineered to better withstand climate change—a definite advantage to the technology. However, others have pointed out that reduced biodiversity caused by GMO crops could actually worsen the problem. Do you see a way around this dilemma?

2. The last viewpoint in this chapter was written 20 years ago. What aspects of the discussion so far does this piece seem to be missing? Based on this piece, how has the debate about GMOs evolved over the decades?

Chapter 3

1. The second viewpoint in this chapter argues that hunger is a complex issue, and lack of adequate nutrition is not limited to people who do not have enough to eat. How can hunger be seen as an issue of "politics and justice"? How are potential solutions different when hunger is seen in this way?

2. In this chapter's viewpoint by Million Belay, the author points out that GM crops in Africa would take control of the food system out of the hands of African farmers and put it in the hands of American agrobusiness companies. Is this similar to colonization? Why or why not?

Chapter 4

1. In this first viewpoint in this chapter, author Colin Tudge suggests that well-designed cities can play a role in addressing vitamin deficiencies. He doesn't offer details. Can you think of ways cities might be designed to help residents grow nutritious foods?

2. While decisions about what foods to buy are quite personal, the viewpoints in this chapter have shown that there are many large corporations with deep and vested interests in what foods you eat. After reading this chapter, has your view about control of the food supply changed? Why or why not?

Organizations to Contact

The editors have compiled the following list of organizations concerned with the issues debated in this book. The descriptions are derived from materials provided by the organizations. All have publications or information available for interested readers. The list was compiled on the date of publication of the present volume; the information provided here may change. Be aware that many organizations take several weeks or longer to respond to inquiries, so allow as much time as possible.

Biodiversity International

Via dei Tre Denari, 472/a
00054 Maccarese (Fiumicino), Italy
(39-06) 61181
email: Biodiversity@cgiar.org
website: www.bioversityinternational.org

Biodiversity International delivers scientific evidence, management practices and policy options to safeguard agricultural and tree biodiversity to attain sustainable global food and nutrition security.

Center for Food Safety

660 Pennsylvania Avenue SE, #302
Washington, DC 20003
(202) 547-9359
email: office@centerforfoodsafety.org
website: www.centerforfoodsafety.org

Center for Food Safety (CFS) is a national nonprofit public interest and environmental advocacy organization working to protect human health and the environment by curbing the use of harmful food production technologies and by promoting organic and other forms of sustainable agriculture.

Food and Agriculture Organization of the United Nations

Viale delle Terme di Caracalla
00153 Rome, Italy
(+39) 06 57051
email: FAO-HQ@fao.org
website: www.Fao.org/home/en/

The Food and Agriculture Organization of the United Nations (FAO) leads international efforts to defeat hunger, by working to create a world free of hunger and malnutrition where food and agriculture contribute to improving the living standards of all, especially the poorest, in an economically, socially, and environmentally sustainable manner.

Genetic Literacy Project

8 West 126th Street
Suite 3B119
New York, NY 10027
(410) 941-9374
email: info@geneticliteracyproject.org
website: www.Geneticliteracyproject.org

The Genetic Literacy Project, a part of the Science Literacy Project, explores the intersection of DNA research and real world applications of genetics with the media and policy worlds in order to disentangle science from ideology. The commitment of the GLP is to promote public awareness and constructive discussion of genetics, biotechnology, evolution, and science literacy.

International Federation of Organic Agriculture Movements (IFOAM)

Charles-de-Gaulle-Str. 5
53113 Bonn
Germany
(503) 235 7532 (US phone)
email: D.Gould@ifoam.bio
website: www.ifoam.bio

IFOAM is an umbrella organization of groups supporting organic food and agriculture in 117 nations. It works to facilitate production and trade and promote sustainability in agriculture and help build the capacity of leaders in the organic movement.

The Non GMO Project

Contact via website form
(360) 255-7704
website: www.Nongmoproject.org

The Non GMO Project is a non-profit organization committed to building and protecting the food supply primarily through consumer education and outreach.

Organic Consumers Association

6771 South Silver Hill Drive
Finland, MN 55603
218-226-4164
website: www.Organicconsumers.org

The OCA is a non-profit dedicated to protecting the right of consumers to safe, healthy, and nutritious food, while also ensuring a just food and farming system that respects the environment and biodiversity.

Organic Federation of Canada

12-4475, Grand boulevard
Montreal, QC H4B 2X7
Canada
(514) 488-6192
email: info@organicfederation.ca
website: www.organicfederation.ca

The Organic Federation of Canada brings together all the key players in Canada's organic industry to ensure excellent standards and regulations that stimulate the growth of Canada's organic sector and offer information to help consumers identify organic products.

Rodale Institute

611 Siegfriedale Road
Kutztown, PA 19530-9320 USA
(610) 683-1400
email: info@rodaleinstitute.org
website: www.rodaleinstitute.org

The Rodale Institute works with individual growers at every level. They train farmers interested in organic agriculture, support conventional farmers in transition and work to ensure that all organic farmers are as efficient and economically viable as possible. In addition, the Rodale Institute works with cities and organizations to create viable opportunities for the next generation of organic farmers.

United States Department of Agriculture/ Agricultural Law Information Partnership

National Agricultural Library
10301 Baltimore Avenue
Beltsville, MD 20705
(301) 504-5755
website: www.nal.usda.gov/aglaw/agricultural-law-information-partnership

The Agricultural Law Information Partnership is a collaboration between the National Agricultural Library, National Agricultural Law Center (NALC) and the Center for Agriculture and Food Systems (CAFS) at Vermont Law School. The Partnership supports the dissemination of agricultural and food law information to consumers, researchers and legal professionals. Agricultural law is defined broadly to include land-based agriculture, food and fiber production and systems, aquaculture, and energy issues.

Bibliography of Books

Kelly A. Clancy, *The Politics of Genetically Modified Organisms in the United States and Europe*, New York, NY: Palgrave McMillan, 2017.

Mitchel Cohen, ed. *The Fight Against Monsanto's Roundup: The Politics of Pesticides*, New York, NY: Skyhorse, 2019.

Steven M. Druker, *Altered Genes, Twisted Truth: How the Venture to Genetically Engineer Our Food Has Subverted Science, Corrupted Government, and Systematically Deceived the Public,* Salt Lake City, UT: Clear River Press, 2015.

Jessica Eise and Ken Foster, eds., *How to Feed the World*, Washington, DC: Island Press, 2018.

Carey Gillam, *Whitewash: The Story of a Weed Killer, Cancer, and the Corruption of Science*, Washington, DC: Island Press, 2017.

McKay Jenkins, *Food Fight: The Future of the American Diet,* New York: Random House, 2017.

Barbara Krasner, *The Food Chain: Regulation, Inspection, and Supply*, New York, NY: Cavendish Square, 2019.

Sheldon Krimsky, *GMOs Decoded: A Skeptic's View of GMO Foods*, Cambridge, MA: MIT Press, 2019.

Amanda Little, *The Fate of Food: What We'll Eat in a Bigger, Hotter, Smarter World*, New York, NY: Harmony, 2019.

Mark Lynas, *Seeds of Science: Why We Got it So Wrong on GMOs*, London, UK: Bloomsbury, 2018.

Megan Mitchell, *Genetically Modified Crops*, New York, NY: Cavendish Square, 2019.

Marion Nestle, *Unsavory Truth: How Food Companies Skew the Science of What We Eat*, New York: Basic, 2018.

Ed Regis, *Golden Rice: The Imperiled Birth of a GMO Superfood*, Baltimore, MD: Johns Hopkins University Press, 2019.

David Rieff, *The Reproach of Hunger: Food, Justice, and Money in the Twenty-First Century*, New York, NY; Simon and Schuster, 2016.

Robert D. Saik, *Food 5.0: How We Feed the Future*, Austin, TX: Lioncrest, 2019.

Vandana Shiva, *Who Really Feeds the World: The Failtures of Agribusiness and the Promise of Agroecology*, Berkeley, CA: North Atlantic Books, 2016.

Timothy A. Wise, *Eating Tomorrow: Agribusiness, Family Farmers, and the Battle for the Future of Food*, New York, NY: The New Press, 2019.

Index

A

Africa, 31, 47, 84, 106–109, 123

Agent Orange, 73

agroecology, explanation of, 96, 98–100

Ann, Melis, 33–39

AquaBounty salmon, 118

Arctic apples, 19–21, 23–24, 118

B

bananas, genetically biofortified, 92, 93–94

Bayer, 15, 135–139, 147, 149

Belay, Million, 106–109, 123

Besley, John C., 140–144

Best Food Facts, 51–56

beta-carotene, 93, 94, 125, 126, 128

Bhargave, Pushpa, 36

Biello, David, 61–64

biodiversity, GMOs as encouraging, 65–69

Borlaug, Norman, 112

bovine growth hormone (rBGH), 155–156

broadforking, 78

Bt crops, 29–31, 34, 41, 46, 47, 68, 73, 83, 93, 97

C

cadaverine, 41

Campbell's, 144, 150

cancer
  GM foods as possible cause of, 40–44
  GM foods as possible preventative for, 42–43

Cassidy, Emily, 66–67

Center for Food Safety, 22

C4 photosynthesis, 28, 29, 104–105

Chassy, Bruce, 52, 53, 54, 55

climate change, how GM crops can withstand effects of, 16, 69, 72, 75–79, 90, 101–105, 123, 158–161

confined animal feeding operations (CAFOs), 100

Cooperative Wheat Research and Production Program, 112

corn, and bacteria genes, 22, 34, 46, 68

corn borer, 68

cotton, genetically modified variety of, 29–30, 35, 46, 47, 108

Council for Biotechnology Information, 114–115

cover crops, 77

Crick, Francis, 15

CRISPR, 20, 21, 23, 73, 74, 103, 137

crop regulation, guidelines for GM foods, 45–50

Crop Trust, 72

cross pollination, 70, 74

D

Deb, Debal, 136, 137, 139

deoxyribonucleic acid (DNA), discovery of structure of, 15

Diehl, Paul, 117–120

Dixon, Graham, 140–144

Dow Chemical, 73, 136, 149, 155

drought tolerance/resistance, 69, 97, 108, 139

DuPont, 118, 136, 147, 149

E

EMBRAPA, 94

European Network of Scientists for Social and Environmental Responsibility (ENSSER), 127, 134

F

farming, as causing reduction in biodiversity, 65, 67–68

fish, and cattle growth genes, 22

Fisher, Kiley, 149

Flavr-Savr Tomato, 118

folate, 94

Franklin, Rosalind, 15

G

General Mills, 141, 150

genetically modified (GM) crops/foods

how corporate control of GM crops affects the food supply, 110–116, 122–123, 124–134, 135–139, 140–144, 145–151, 152–157, 158–161

how they affect the environment, 59–60, 61–64, 65–69, 70–74, 75–79, 80–87

safety of, 17–18, 19–24, 25–32, 33–39, 40–44, 45–50, 51–56

as solution to combatting global hunger, 25–32, 80–87, 89–90, 91–95, 96–100, 101–105, 106–109, 110–116, 117–120, 158–161

Genetic Literacy Project, 110–116

Ghorashi, Mahmi, 145–148, 150–151

Giovannetti, Marco, 65–69

glufosinate, 64, 73

glyphosate, 15, 18, 21, 40, 41–44, 64, 66, 67, 70, 71, 72, 73, 102

Golden Rice, 48, 92, 93, 94, 95, 105, 124, 125–126

Green America, 96–100

Green Revolution, 106, 107, 112, 159

H

health risks, associated with GM foods, 33–39, 40–44

Herrera-Estrella, Luis R., 80–87

I

India, 26, 29, 30, 31, 47, 108

Irish potato famine, 102

ISA Brown chickens, 42

K

Karim, Ghiselle, 152–157

L

labeling, guidelines for GM foods, 19–21, 23–24, 140–144, 145–151
Lemaux, Peggy, 51, 52–53
Liberty, 64
L-tryptophan, 37
Lynas, Mark, 126–127

M

Mars, 150
Martin-Abel, Shirley, 70–74
McComas, Katherine, 140–144
meat consumption, as source of global food demand, 27, 100
monarch butterflies, reduction in population, 67
Monsanto, 15, 35, 36, 41, 44, 62, 63, 64, 66, 110, 118, 135–139, 147, 149, 150, 153, 154, 155, 156, 157
Moore, Nola, 128–129

N

Naam, Ramez, 25–32
Newell-McGloughlin, Martina, 51, 52, 54, 55
nitrogen use efficiency, 97–98
Norero, Daniel, 91–95
North Dakota, 62, 63

O

obesity, 100
organic gardening, how GM crops affect, 70–74, 75–79

P

papaya, 35
Parrott, Wayne, 51, 52, 53, 55
Paterson, Owen, 107, 109, 125
Pauling, Linus, 15
Perls, Dana, 19–21, 23–24
permanent bed system, 78
Philippines, 26, 31
pleiotropy, explanation of, 73
Pollan, Michael, 66
powdery mildew, 103
putrescine, 41

Q

Qaim, Matin, 45–50

R

regenerative agriculture, explanation of, 75–79, 99
rice, genetically biofortified, 48, 92, 93, 94, 95, 105, 124, 125–126, 128, 139
RNA interference, 20
Roundup, 18, 21, 40–44, 64, 66, 71, 149, 154, 156, 157

S

Safe and Accurate Food Labeling Act of 2015, 150

salmon, genetically engineered with eel genes, 20, 118, 146

self-fertilizing crops, 28

sheet composting, 78

Simplot's Innate Potato, 104

Smith, Jeffrey, 40–44

sodium ion (NA+), 160

soil solarization, 78–79

Spring, Kate, 75–79

stacked traits, explanation of, 62

succession planting, 77

"super" pigs, 22

"superweeds," 70, 71, 149, 154

Syngenta, 118, 125, 136, 149

synthetic vanilla, 20, 23

T

terminator seeds, 153, 154

Tester, Mark, 158–161

Thompson, Stuart, 101–105

tomatoes, and flounder genes, 22

transgenic canola plants, as invasive species, 61–64

Tudge, Colin, 124–134

V

Vermont, labeling laws in, 141, 150

Vidal, John, 135–139

W

water use efficiency (WUE), 98

Watson, James, 15

wheat blast, 103

Williams, Maurice, 15

Y

Yee, Aubrey, 42–43

yield gap, methods for closing between rich and poor countries, 27–28